Praise for the Novels of Rhonda Woodward

Moonlight and Mischief

"With its nicely nuanced characters, richly satisfying love story, and graceful writing, Woodward's splendid tale will delight any Regency fan." —*Booklist*

"A very good traditional Regency, with interesting, multi-dimensional characters and plenty of sexual tension." —All About Romance

The Wagered Heart

"A very likable heroine and historically accurate writing that shines . . . enjoyable." —All About Romance

"Remember the name Rhonda Woodward, because this author is developing into a top-flight Regency favorite." —*Romantic Times* (4 stars)

A Spinster's Luck

"Woodward gives romance readers much to enjoy. . . . The tale flows smoothly and naturally, with several refreshingly different plot twists, and the ending is thoroughly satisfying." —Romance Reviews Today

"Talented newcomer Rhonda Woodward [has] penned an enjoyable tale with a mix of mischief and matrimony." —*Romantic Times*

D0645460

REGENCY ROMANCE
COMING IN JANUARY 2006

Rake's Ransom and *A Loyal Companion*
by Barbara Metzger
Together for the first time, two stories of passion from
one of Regency's biggest stars.

0-451-21793-4

Lord Ryburn's Apprentice
by Laurie Bishop
After years of bad luck, Georgiana Marland strikes gold
when a rich relative takes her in. Unaccustomed to the
norms of the ton, however, Georgiana finds herself in
need of instruction—and infatuated with her tutor.

0-451-21731-4

The Ruby Ghost
by June Calvin
Penelope recognizes the home of her new employ-
ers—a castle from an eerie recurring dream. Other
bothers include ghosts and a rakish family relation
who rubs her the wrong way. That is, until he
determines to show her his true colors—and protect
her at all costs.

0-451-21011-5

Available wherever books are sold or at penguin.com

Lady Emma's Dilemma

Rhonda Woodward

A SIGNET BOOK

SIGNET
Published by New American Library, a division of
Penguin Group (USA) Inc., 375 Hudson Street,
New York, New York 10014, USA
Penguin Group (Canada), 90 Eglinton Avenue East, Suite 700, Toronto,
Ontario M4P 2Y3, Canada (a division of Pearson Penguin Canada Inc.)
Penguin Books Ltd., 80 Strand, London WC2R 0RL, England
Penguin Ireland, 25 St. Stephen's Green, Dublin 2,
Ireland (a division of Penguin Books Ltd.)
Penguin Group (Australia), 250 Camberwell Road, Camberwell, Victoria 3124,
Australia (a division of Pearson Australia Group Pty. Ltd.)
Penguin Books India Pvt. Ltd., 11 Community Centre, Panchsheel Park,
New Delhi - 110 017, India
Penguin Group (NZ), cnr Airborne and Rosedale Roads, Albany,
Auckland 1310, New Zealand (a division of Pearson New Zealand Ltd.)
Penguin Books (South Africa) (Pty.) Ltd., 24 Sturdee Avenue,
Rosebank, Johannesburg 2196, South Africa

Penguin Books Ltd., Registered Offices:
80 Strand, London WC2R 0RL, England

First published by Signet, an imprint of New American Library,
a division of Penguin Group (USA) Inc.

First Printing, December 2005
10 9 8 7 6 5 4 3 2 1

Copyright © Rhonda Woodward, 2005
All rights reserved

 REGISTERED TRADEMARK—MARCA REGISTRADA

Printed in the United States of America

Without limiting the rights under copyright reserved above, no part of this publication
may be reproduced, stored in or introduced into a retrieval system, or transmitted, in
any form, or by any means (electronic, mechanical, photocopying, recording, or otherwise), without the prior written permission of both the copyright owner and the
above publisher of this book.

PUBLISHER'S NOTE
This is a work of fiction. Names, characters, places, and incidents either are the prod-
uct of the author's imagination or are used fictitiously, and any resemblance to actual
persons, living or dead, business establishments, events, or locales is entirely coinci-
dental.
    The publisher does not have any control over and does not assume any respon-
sibility for author or third-party Web sites or their content.

If you purchased this book without a cover you should be aware that this book is stolen
property. It was reported as "unsold and destroyed" to the publisher and neither the author nor the publisher has received any payment for this "stripped book."

The scanning, uploading, and distribution of this book via the Internet or via any other
means without the permission of the publisher is illegal and punishable by law. Please
purchase only authorized electronic editions, and do not participate in or encourage
electronic piracy of copyrighted materials. Your support of the author's rights is appreciated.

Chapter One

1817

"Well, if I am going to take a lover, I had best meet a few gentlemen," Lady Emmaline Fallbrook declared in a flawlessly serene tone of voice.

"Emmaline!" the dowager Duchess of Kelbourne exclaimed in a sharp whisper, whipping her regal head around quickly to see if the people streaming past their theatre box had heard her granddaughter's outrageous statement.

Keeping her expression calm, Emma gazed at her grandmother with barely suppressed amusement. She knew her comment was outrageously scandalous, but did not care. With a delicious feeling of mischief she watched the play of emotion cross the old lady's surprisingly unlined face.

In truth, it gave her a secret thrill of satisfaction to see her normally imperturbable grandmother's flabbergasted expression. Since she was a child, it had been a great feat to elicit such a reaction from her.

"Did I shock you, Grandmère?" she asked, raising her brows in feigned innocence. "That would be above strange since you have been telling me for years that I have grown dull from too much time spent in my own company."

The dowager's jewels, flashing beneath the light of the chandelier, matched the glint in her perceptive steel blue gaze. "Saying you have kept yourself from Society for far too long is a far cry from suggesting that you take a . . . a . . . I shall not repeat such outrageousness! To make such

an announcement where just anyone might overhear—
Well! I confess myself shocked at you."

Emma reached over and laid her hand upon her grandmother's arm and finally gave way to her suppressed mirth.
"You must forgive me, Grandmère, you know how much I
love to tease you."

As the noise of the crowd, still flooding in from the
streets, reached almost deafening levels, Emma scrutinized
her grandmother's expression.

Despite the good lady's words to the contrary, Emma
could tell that Grandmère was not as shocked as she pre-
tended to be. This knowledge afforded Emma some measure of relief.

Just as Grandmère opened her mouth to reply, the velvet
curtain at the entrance of their box fell aside. An elegant
gray-haired gentleman, dressed completely in black, except
for his parchment white shirt and cravat, stepped in and
made an elegant leg.

"My dear duchess," he intoned, "I cannot express my delight when I glanced up to see that you had decided to treat
us all to your most desirable presence."

"Harwich!" Grandmère cried out like a young girl. "I
wondered if you would be in Town this Season!" She held
out her gloved hand to him.

By the way he lingered over Grandmère's hand, Emma
had a suspicion that the earl had once been one of Grandmère's beaux.

"You remember my granddaughter?" the dowager asked,
sending a look to Emma that showed a great deal of pride.
"Emmaline, I am sure you recall Lord Harwich."

Smiling up at the earl, Emma said, "Indeed I do. I spent
some time with your daughter in Bath last spring and enjoyed her company immensely. I trust that Lady Davinia is
in good health?"

"She is very well, Lady Fallbrook. And I know she certainly enjoyed your company as well. I must say that it is

very good to see you again. I clearly recall the year of your come-out, what, nine or ten years ago?"

"'Tis gone thirteen years, sir," Emma said with a smile.

"Truly? I remember it so vividly. Everyone was agog with your beauty and poise. As they are again."

"You are too kind, Lord Harwich." Feeling the blush come to her cheeks, Emma chided herself for being such a pea goose. Her grandmother may have it right after all; she had allowed herself to become much too provincial and had lost some of her polish.

"Not kind at all. Just yester eve I supped at Lady Colhurst's and half the evening was spent discussing the dash you have already cut through Town."

Grandmère waited long enough for Emma to thank the earl again before tapping him lightly on the wrist with her sandalwood fan. "Unless you have guests waiting for you in your box, why don't you join us?"

Lord Harwich's smile anticipated his answer. "How kind, my dear duchess. As a matter of fact, my guests sent their regrets at the last moment—how exceedingly lucky for me."

The elegant old lady blushed at his gallantry and the earl seated himself on the gilded chair between her and Emma.

As Grandmère and Lord Harwich continued to chat, Emma resumed her perusal of the theatre. The last play she had attended had been with Charles in the early years of their marriage, when she had still been hopeful that they could find something in common to enjoy. However, Charles had hated everything about Town, especially the theater. "A play? Who wants to mix with the rabble?" he used to say whenever she suggested a visit to Drury Lane.

Scanning the luxurious boxes, she realized that they most likely held people she had been well acquainted with years ago. She smiled at the prospect of reestablishing some of those connections.

Shifting restlessly in her chair, she leaned forward slightly to look over the front of the box down to the narrow rows of seats in the pit below. The seats were filling quickly with a colorful assortment of people.

Again, she looked around the large oval space, recalling that the theater had not been nearly this grand ten years ago. The news of the fire that had razed the previous building had even reached her in Yorkshire. This new building, with its impressive domed rotunda, tiers of ornately ornamented boxes and sweeping double staircase in the entrance hall, was a splendid example of the new style of architecture.

As the crowd swelled and the candlelight glinted off the fronts of the gilded boxes, Emma felt excitement fluttering in her stomach.

Why had she waited so long to return to London? she wondered for the hundredth time since arriving in Town three days ago. She had missed the excitement that had always accompanied a Season, and now that she was here, all her previous hesitation seemed ridiculous.

Well, no matter now, she told herself. She was here and she was going to enjoy herself.

"I am probably not the first to inform you, dear Duchess, that Devruex is come to London. He had a prime bit of blood make its first appearance today. The filly beat one of Grafton's favorites by a nose."

At Lord Harwich's words, Emma was pulled from her musings and left reeling in surprise.

Devruex. Her head whipped around to look from Lord Harwich to her grandmother in alarm. Jack Devruex was in London!

Grandmère, the porcelain skin around her blue eyes crinkling with her smile, leaned toward her old friend. "My dear Lord Harwich, I am a day or two ahead of your news. Several of my friends who have unmarried granddaughters are already scrambling to send Lord Devruex invitations. In truth, I doubt their efforts will do much good. Though he usually comes to Town for the Season, Devruex is notorious for shunning the more mundane entertainments. Unless racing, gambling, or fencing is involved, Devruex rarely puts in an appearance in Society."

Harwich chuckled and nodded his gray head. "You are always aware of everything worth knowing, dear Duchess."

"In truth, there are so few young people who interest me, I make sure I know what they are up to," she said. "It keeps me young."

"You are eternally young, m'dear," Lord Harwich said with a warm smile for the dowager.

A wave of cold panic washed over Emma's body.

Frantically scanning the crowds for a tall, black-haired man, Emma gripped the chair arms to prevent her hands from trembling.

He could be anywhere! She craned her neck in an attempt to see into the nearest boxes. Her anxiety rising, she knew she could encounter Jack Devruex at any moment!

Before coming to London, she believed she had prepared herself for such a thing. After all, she had quite gotten over the fact that young Baron Devruex broke her heart thirteen years ago. Now that she faced the very real prospect of seeing him again, she prayed that it would not be tonight.

Foolish, foolish Emmaline, she chided herself. How could she have ever thought that thirteen years would be long enough?

On the verge of pleading a headache so that she could escape, she caught a glimpse of a black-haired gentleman among the crowd below. Her heart leapt with mounting dread.

Half rising from her chair, she hazily formed a plan to leave the theatre box and hide in the cloakroom if need be. An instant later, the dark-haired man turned and the abject relief that he was not Lord Devruex shook her from the grip of panic.

Relaxing back into her chair, she took a deep breath and waited for her heart to slow its frantic pace. She concentrated on keeping her expression pleasant, and on all the

reasons why she had decided to come to London rushed up
to rescue her roiling emotions.

*Good Lord, I'm almost one and thirty, not some missish
schoolgirl!* Finally, she felt her fingers begin to relax, and
she released her painful grip on the chair arms.

Feeling calmer, she reminded herself that she had lived
an entire lifetime in the last thirteen years. She had faced
loss and grief and other situations more onerous than possibly meeting a man who had doubtless given her very little
thought since they had last met.

She had always known if she came to London there was
a strong possibility that she would encounter Jack Devruex.

Nothing had really changed from a moment ago, came
the reassuring thought. Nothing at all. She had a plan and
she would see it through, she reminded herself with determination. She would set aside all her worries about the
past—and the future—and think only of enjoying herself.

Hang Jack Devruex, she thought with relief and renewed
confidence.

Feeling her spirits much restored, she turned back to her
grandmother and stately Lord Harwich. Thankfully, neither
seemed to have noticed her momentary discomfiture.

Hang Jack Devruex, she thought again, and there was a
hint of vehemence in the sentiment. If—or more likely
when—they met again, she would simply give him the
most elegant cut sublime and move on. He certainly de-
served no more from her.

Finally, just as the crowds were growing alarmingly
restive, the heavy curtains drew back in a great wave from
the stage. The orchestra, hidden from view in the pits,
struck up a lively overture.

The audience quieted and the play began. But after several minutes, to Emma's great disappointment, the company displayed rather indifferent talent in a confusing
comedy having something vaguely to do with mistaken
identity.

Soon, she found her mind, as well as her gaze, wandering from the stage. Scanning the other theatregoers, she thought many of them more diverting than the play. To her amusement, she noticed most of them following her suit— watching the notables rather than the rather dull show.

Though the actors struggled to be heard over the noise of the restive crowd, Emma still found the whole scene excessively entertaining. It had been so long since she had experienced this kind of excitement.

Then, as suddenly as the closing of a music box, the noise of the crowd ceased. Emma glanced back to the stage in surprise. Even the actors seemed to falter in confusion.

"What is happening?" Grandmère demanded, raising her lorgnette to get a better look at the stage.

Gripping the warm wooden armrests, Emma looked around the packed theatre, sensing the excitement and a palpable feeling of anticipation emanating from the crowd.

"Is the Prince Regent joining us tonight?" Emma could think of no other reason for this odd scene.

Grandmère gave an inelegant snort. "Tosh. No one gets that excited over fat little Prinny." She continued using the lorgnette to peruse the crowd with curiosity.

"I suspect . . ." Lord Harwich began, squinting in the direction of a box not much removed from theirs. "Yes! Mrs. Willoughby has arrived," he announced.

Grandmère immediately lowered the lorgnette and sat back in her chair with an indignant twitch of her shoulders. "Oh! I shall not look in that direction again!"

"Who in the world is Mrs. Willoughby?" Emma kept her gaze riveted on the box Lord Harwich indicated as a dark-haired woman entered on the arm of a formally dressed gentleman.

Emma observed them with great interest. Even the actors on the stage seemed to be aware of the late arrivals.

The beautiful brunette glided to the front of the box and stood for a moment where she could be seen more easily by the entire theatre.

It was difficult to judge her height, but her slim, graceful figure gave the impression of regal tallness. Her dark hair, arranged in a riot of ringlets artfully erupting from a toque, must have taken her maid hours to perfect. Her claret-and cream-colored gown revealed an elegant expanse of alabaster décolletage.

Even from this distance, Emma saw that her complexion gleamed pale and flawless beneath the thousands of candles, and her lips were glossy crimson.

Emma, who had inherited a fondness for jewels from her mother and grandmother, took note of the glittering collar of rubies, or garnets, encircling Mrs. Willoughby's neck. A brooch with the same stone the size of a pigeon's egg rested in a gather of silk between her breasts.

Emma continued to observe the mysterious woman, fascinated by the manner in which the crowd seemed to be holding their collective breaths at her appearance. Mrs. Willoughby stood above them like a queen accepting tribute from her subjects.

"Who is she?" She directed her question to the earl, who cast Grandmère a hesitant look, as if seeking her permission to speak.

Turning her nose up with a sniff, Grandmère said, "I am sure the subject of Mrs. Willoughby cannot be avoided for long. It is bad enough that the cits and hoi polloi speak of nothing else, but her name is on the lips of half the *ton* as well. And I cannot see why. I will own that she is an attractive woman, but certainly nothing out of the most common way. My granddaughter's beauty outshines hers tenfold."

Lord Harwich inclined his head. "I agree. Lady Fallbrook has no rival in beauty, but Mrs. Willoughby has no rival in infamy."

"Please, Lord Harwich, though I could happily listen to your compliments all evening, I am exceedingly curious about the mysterious Mrs. Willoughby." Emma glanced back to see that the woman had finally taken the seat next to her escort.

"It's a shocking tale, Lady Fallbrook, though everyone

knows of it. Mrs. Willoughby burst on the scene last Season in some utterly forgettable opera. Soon Lord Monteford, old Pellerton's heir . . . er . . . befriended her. Shortly thereafter, she quit the theatre and started appearing all over town, driving a bright red carriage with white ponies, wearing a different set of jewels every day."

Grandmère abandoned her indifferent pose and tapped her fan sharply on her chair arm. "She is a woman given over to a shameful want of decency and decorum. Monteford's mama, an old friend of mine, has taken to her bed over the fortune he has squandered on that wanton." She glared at the box despite her earlier avowal not to look in that direction again.

"Is there a Mr. Willoughby?" Emma asked the earl.

"No one seems to know for sure. But there is a rumor that Monteford pays a bit of blunt to keep him snug in the country."

"Despite her queenly demeanor, she is a wretched creature who does not even have the decency to be discreet in her depravity," Grandmère put in.

Emma continued to watch Mrs. Willoughby and Lord Monteford. "Indeed, the better part of depravity is discretion."

Lord Harwich chuckled at this quip and Grandmère scowled.

"She is exceedingly beautiful," Emma continued. Though she was certainly not naïve about the ways of the world, she had never seen a mistress of a member of Polite Society show herself so openly in public. She found herself quite curious about Mrs. Willoughby, marveling at how the woman obviously enjoyed her notoriety.

"Yes. All of London has fallen under her spell. Crowds follow her and a day rarely passes without mention of her in the gossip papers," Lord Harwich replied.

How daring, how fascinating, Emma mused, before turning her attention to Mrs. Willoughby's companion,

Lord Monteford. He seemed to take no notice of the crowd's attention and kept his impassive gaze on the stage.

To be sure, he was a rather impressive-looking gentleman. His pale brown hair was swept back from a nobly proportioned forehead. His features were handsome in the classical mode. The only flaw she noted—saving him from being almost pretty—was his rather thin lips. His build was above slim, though athletic, and his superbly cut evening clothes accented his shoulders.

As for his whole demeanor, she observed, he came off a bit proud, but that may have only been due to having to keep his chin lifted above his high collar, she surmised charitably.

As she did her best to watch Mrs. Willoughby and Lord Monteford inconspicuously, Grandmère and Lord Harwich conversed quietly and turned their attention back to the play.

After another moment, Emma followed their suit only to see that the play had not improved. She allowed her attention to wander again. Most of the crowd attended to their own conversations and gawked at Mrs. Willoughby. The players on stage could barely be heard above the restless din.

Suddenly, the lead actor caught Emma's attention by doing something quite strange.

He moved to the middle of the stage and remained completely still and quiet even though it was apparent that the next line was his. After a moment, as people began to take notice and quiet down, he turned away from the leading lady and faced the audience.

As the other actors looked at one another nervously, he moved forward to the edge of the stage, finally gaining the full attention of the spectators.

Emma exchanged a curious glance with her grandmother, but the old lady's shrug showed that she was just as confused by the actor's odd behavior.

Whatever his intention, the effect was quite dramatic.

Emma watched the man, fascinated to see what he would do next.

"Indeed, Gwendolyn," he suddenly spoke in a tone that carried throughout the theatre, addressing the audience rather than the confused actress playing Gwendolyn. "There are few to rival you in beauty."

His voice rose as he spread his arms wide before continuing, a mischievous smile spreading across his face.

"Our own Queen Willow has reigned supreme for a Season or two, thrilling us all with the ethereal beauty of her person," he began in a baritone voice filled with mock gravity. "But the sudden arrival of a *true lady from the north*— whose enchanting splendor and effortless charm captured our admiration so quickly—may well dethrone Queen Willow from our hearts. We, their humble subjects, can only wait and watch with delight for what may happen next." He lifted both arms up, gesturing dramatically toward the boxes holding Mrs. Willoughby and Emma.

Collectively, the crowd gasped in shock at this unusual departure from the play, then let out a tremendous roar of excitement.

Astonished, Emma watch as hundreds of heads turned to look up and stare from her to Mrs. Willoughby, clapping and stamping their feet in approval of the actor's impromptu speech.

Emma froze, unable to look at her grandmother or Lord Harwich, for there was no mistaking that the actor referred to her as the *true lady from the north*.

After a few choked gasps and splutters, Grandmère finally found her voice and said, "This is an outrage! I shall have a word with the manager about this—sink me if I don't!"

The rumbling applause grew so loud the very walls seemed to vibrate.

"Please allow me the honor of making the complaint for you, Duchess. I shall know how to deal with such impertinence," Lord Harwich stated in an attempt to soothe the dowager's outrage.

"How dare that turnip place a reference to my granddaughter in the same sentence with that trollop—just to divert the lower classes from this wretched play! Such insolence is inexcusable!" Grandmère's outrage could not be assuaged.

In her astonishment and confusion, Emma glanced over to the box Mrs. Willoughby occupied. To her surprise, the woman was looking directly at her. The anger in her gaze was plain even from this distance and the intensity of the glare was startling.

Emma quickly pulled her gaze away and immediately met Lord Monteford's eyes. The amused twist to his lips showed that he had not taken offense at the actor's cheeky conduct. His smile widened as he held her gaze, until she lifted her chin slightly and looked away.

To her utter relief, the curtain finally fell on the first act. However, the crowd did not cease its deafening cheer.

"Shall we leave, Grandmère?" Emma asked. She had never found herself the object of such public scrutiny and felt completely at a loss as what to do.

"We shall not! Indeed, why should we leave? We shall stare this rabble out of countenance and stand our ground."

Lord Harwich slapped his knee. "That's the way to do it, Duchess! Just like you to face things out. And I see your granddaughter takes after you. We shall ignore this noisy horde and show them how their betters behave."

Emma could not help but smile at Lord Harwich's enthusiasm and felt some of her shock at receiving such unwanted attention dissolve.

Her upbringing had instilled in her a deep abhorrence of any kind of public attention, but that same demanding schooling had given her the effortless ability to keep her composure no matter the inner conflict.

Keenly aware of the staring crowd, she opened her fan

and began to use it on her cheeks in a desultory fashion, her expression serene.

To her surprise, the crowd applauded even more vigorously.

Feeling almost painfully self-conscious, she reminded herself that her sole purpose in coming to London was to leave her dull life behind for a while.

Well, she was certainly off to a good start, she mused, keeping her gaze fixed on the stage as the crowd continued to cheer.

Chapter Two

A fine rain misted the tree-lined lane and the crier bellowed half past midnight as Jack Devruex was admitted into Mrs. Willoughby's elegant townhouse by her equally elegant butler.

"Good evening, my lord," the thin man intoned as he took Jack's hat and gloves. "Mrs. Willoughby and his lordship are in the drawing room with the rest of their guests."

"Thank you, Rivers, no need to announce me." Long strides took him through the entryway and up the stairs, for he knew his way around Sally Willoughby's house quite well. He whistled as he strolled along the narrow hallway, feeling quite satisfied with the world this night.

After an arduous harvest and an even more challenging winter, he'd been more than ready to leave the cares of his estates to his managers while he concentrated on his real interests. His plan was proceeding in an exceedingly satisfactory manner evidenced by the raucous evening he had just spent celebrating the success of a promising filly.

The horse, a three-year-old he had sensed was special from the week of her birth, had performed incredibly well today in an informal race against the Duke of Grafton's favorite new bit of blood.

He slapped his fist into his palm in satisfaction at the memory. By damn, but Circes loved to run. More than that, she could not stand to trail behind any other horse in the field. She had stamina, heart and that indefinable something that told him she could be a winner.

Even Grafton—whose monumental success as a thoroughbred breeder Jack desired to emulate—had been impressed with the chestnut thoroughbred, and lingered after the race to discuss breeding programs and training theories.

Barring the unexpected, and Providence knew that in horse breeding the unexpected was the normal mode of things, Circes had the stuff to win the Severly Stakes next month. If she did, the future of his stud would be secured. Winning the Severly meant everything.

But for now, he would conclude his revelry by spending the end of it with a few old friends at Sal Willoughby's townhouse.

As he approached the drawing room he could hear loud laughter even from this distance.

A sleepy footman bowed and opened the door to a sumptuously decorated sitting room. Jack stepped in and saw the familiar swags of maroon and gold velvet draping the windows. Braces of candles sputtered low in their sockets and a faintly sweet, musky scent lay heavy in the air. This and the numerous cushions and pillows strewn about gave the room a vaguely decadent, haremlike feel. How like Sally Willoughby to have even her drawing room reflect her sensual personality.

He saw that in addition to Sally and Monteford, Lords Darley and Bellingham and Mrs. Pennyworth also lounged around the room. Jack took note of the empty bottle of champagne on a table next to the beautiful Sally Willoughby. He also saw a number of empty bottles of port discarded near the other guests.

Conversation ceased as everyone turned at his entry and he performed a casual bow to his hostess. "Good evening, dear Sal. It looks as if I have a bit of catching up to do," he said, with a droll glance toward the spent bottles.

"Devruex!" Sally cried in pleasure. Jumping up, she quickly crossed the room to curtsy to the baron. "I knew you would come! Your friends said that you had no doubt found other amusements, but I knew you would not go back on your promise to visit."

She put her hand in the crook of his elbow and drew him farther into the room as the others rose from their sprawling poses on the various pieces of furniture.

"Evening, Monteford," Jack said after greeting the others.

A hint of a smile lurked in the corner of his old friend's mouth as he returned the greeting. "How like you to arrive just when we are about to broach another bottle of brandy."

"Indeed!" Lord Darley agreed before Jack could respond. "I was just saying that it was too bad that Devruex's not here to enjoy this fine vintage—and in you walk!"

"Must be clairvoyant, Darley," fat Lord Bellingham declared from his place next to the blond Mrs. Pennyworth.

"Clairvoyant!" Mrs. Pennyworth screeched and went off into gales of giggles for no apparent reason.

Sally, looking exquisitely beautiful in a claret-and-cream-colored gown that flattered her pale complexion, handed Jack a snifter filled with a generous portion of brandy and gestured to the chair next to hers.

The expression in her dark eyes as they held his told him more than words could how pleased she was to see him. The smile he sent her in return was polite but subdued. He certainly had no desire to poach his friend's mistress, no matter how many sultry looks the lovely Mrs. Willoughby sent him.

He leaned back in the comfortable chair, crossed his ankles and took a satisfying swallow of the amber liquid.

Sally sent him another smile. "We missed your company at the theatre tonight. The play was quite unexceptional, but it would have been ever so much better to have had your sharp and amusing observations to divert us."

"It's nice to be missed," Jack said, acknowledging the compliment by lofting his glass in her direction.

"Yes, you should have been there, Devruex. One of the

demmed actors got some maggot in his brain and diverted from the script."

By the amused look Monteford shot Sally as he spoke, and the sour look she sent him in return, Jack suspected there was much more to the story.

With an angry wave of her hand, Sally said, "That wretched creature! How dare he suggest some oddly garbed woman could rival me in any way."

A flash of annoyance crossed Monteford's features, but he remained slouched on the sofa, rolling his glass of brandy between his hands. "Well, my love, that oddly garbed woman is the Lady Fallbrook, and she is an extremely wealthy widow, as well as strikingly beautiful."

Sally sent the viscount such a look of vexation that Jack raised a brow and Lord Bellingham and Mrs. Pennyworth exchanged knowing glances.

Monteford grinned at his mistress' mute fury. "But of course, yours is a beauty that has no rival, my love."

Jack saw with amusement that Sally did not seem at all mollified by Monteford's halfheartedly offered olive branch.

He was about to offer his own compliment when Monteford's words suddenly sank in.

Lady Fallbrook. The words seemed to reverberate through his body. He tightened his grip on the glass before it could slip from his suddenly lax fingers.

"Did you say Lady Emmaline Fallbrook?" Even to his own ears his tone sounded sharp.

Monteford raised his brows at Jack's question. "Yes. She has not been to Town in ages even though she was widowed five or six years ago."

Emmaline Fallbrook. For an instant, the last thirteen years vanished and a vision of sea blue eyes, thick light brown hair, a swanlike neck, and the sound of deep, bubbling laughter besieged Jack's senses.

"Lady Fallbrook?" Mrs. Pennyworth slurred the name from her half-prone position on the sofa. "Someone pointed her out to me in the park t'other day. Everyone was commenting on the striking style of her habit."

Lord Darley uncrossed his legs, sat up, and pushed his flaxen hair off his forehead. "I too saw Lady Fallbrook in the park. Exquisite creature! You will think me incredibly clever when I tell you that I ferreted out the information that the perfectly perfect Lady Fallbrook will be attending Lady Colhurst's ball tomorrow night. Make no doubt that I shall make it my business to be there. And I shall have no problem gaining an introduction, for her granny and mine have known each other since they were babes."

Sally Willoughby gave a loud sniff. "I grant you that she is an attractive woman, but I did not notice anything out of the ordinary way."

Darley pushed himself further up in his chair and a beatific smile spread across his features. "Attractive? My dear Sally, I would describe Lady Fallbrook as magnificently elegant, incomparably graceful, with a visage that may be more hauntingly striking than classically beautiful, but I would never use such a weak word as attractive."

"Lady Fallbrook, you say? I don't believe I am acquainted with any Fallbrooks," Lord Bellingham said as Mrs. Pennyworth refilled his glass from the half-empty bottle next to her chair.

"Lady Fallbrook was formerly Lady Emmaline Wenlock," Monteford supplied.

"Wenlock?" Bellingham asked. "Ah, then the lady is the Duke of Kelbourne's sister. How very interesting."

Jack remained motionless, allowing the conversation to whirl around him as he struggled to regain control of his roiling thoughts.

Even so, he could not miss the sharp look Sally sent Monteford before she said to them all in a breezy tone, "Goodness, I shall have to take a closer look next time I chance to be in Lady Fallbrook's presence. Her ensemble was certainly unique. I pride myself on keeping up on the very latest modes of fashion, but I have never seen anything quite like the gown she wore this evening."

There was something in Sally's tone that made it clear that her words were not meant to be a compliment.

"Yes, she is extremely fashionable and has quite elegant manners. I shall do my best to claim the first waltz with her tomorrow night. I have every intention of developing an acquaintance with the lovely widow," Darley said and took another gulp from his glass.

With an air of amused indulgence, Monteford said, "I commend you on your decisiveness, my friend."

As if galvanized by some unseen force, Jack abruptly pushed himself from his chair and stalked to the fireplace. Placing a foot on the fender he stared into the empty grate as the others continued to gossip about Lady Fallbrook. Running long fingers through his hair, he allowed the truth of the last few moments to sink in.

So she has come to London at last.

After tossing back half his brandy, he shook his head in sharp self-disgust. He felt ridiculous having this extreme reaction to the news that Emmaline had come to Town. It felt rather like being hit in the stomach.

He reminded himself that life had continued during the last thirteen years, and it had continued in a most satisfactory manner. There had always been the likelihood that they would meet again and he thought he had ceased to be concerned about it long ago.

"And what has you looking so pensive, sir?"

Sally's softly spoken question pulled him from his thoughts and he turned to see her gazing up at him. The flickering candle glow did nothing to conceal the curious—and ardent—gleam in her fine eyes.

He was about to make an offhand reply when Monteford spoke up from his place on the sofa.

"Yes, why are you not throwing out your usual bon mots, Devruex? Hold on." He sat up and placed his snifter on the small end table. "Something about all this is vaguely familiar. I seem to recall a similar evening, years ago, when we spoke of Lady Emmaline."

With determined effort, Jack kept his expression placid as his old friend narrowed his eyes in concentration.

If Monteford were not so disguised by the amount of brandy he had consumed, Jack knew the viscount would have no trouble recalling that sultry night long ago when they had last spoken of Lady Emmaline.

He fervently hoped that his old friend would not suddenly regain his memory at this particular moment. He was not prepared to fend off the inevitable questions if Monteford recalled the time when, thirteen years ago, Jack had proclaimed his intention of running away with Lady Emmaline Wenlock.

"Oh, bother Lady Fallbrook," Sally said with more than a hint of temper in her tone. "I for one have heard enough about her for an evening. Do not you agree, Ivy?"

"Lud, yes," Mrs. Pennyworth agreed.

Jack felt some of the tension leave his shoulders, even though Monteford still gazed at him with slightly narrowed eyes. Obviously, he was still racking his brain about Lady Fallbrook.

Jack held Monteford's gaze until Sally introduced some other bit of gossip, finally distracting Monteford from the vexing subject of Lady Fallbrook.

Unfortunately, Jack's thoughts could not be so easily diverted.

So Emmaline Wenlock—no, Lady Fallbrook—has finally come to London. He could not push the thought away.

In years past, at the start of every Season there had been rumors that she was on her way to Town, but nothing had ever come of it.

After the death of Charles Fallbrook and after the appropriate time for mourning had past, there had again been intense speculation that Lady Emmaline would grace London.

Even so, years continued to pass until the *ton* had quite given up on ever seeing her again.

Occasionally, some fashionable fribble would return to Town after spending time with the countess at her country home. They could dine at the best tables for a week on the tales they shared of how Lady Fallbrook lived.

But she never came to London.

Until now.

"Do tell us about your amazing horse, Lord Devruex. Bellingham laid a monkey on the odds for me and I was beside myself when I heard she won," Mrs. Pennyworth called from her place on the sofa.

In one swallow he finished the remainder of his brandy and turned back to the others. Thirteen years was a long time. Much too long to give Emmaline Fallbrook another thought.

Chapter Three

"I have, indeed, rusticated much too long if I am this twit-terpated over a ball," Emma said aloud although she was alone in the room. A small smile came to her lips. Talking to herself was a habit she had developed after living so many years alone. As far as most habits went, she felt this one was rather harmless.

Moving across the sumptuous blue-and-gold bedchamber, she went to the vanity table that stood between two long windows and opened a large, carved wooden case that rested on its highly polished surface. She hummed a happy little tune as she pulled out different pieces of jewelry and contemplated the evening ahead.

Adding to her excitement was a sense of anticipation, for her two dearest friends would also be attending the ball. Amelia Spence-Jones and Penelope, Countess of Tunbridge, had each sent a note over this afternoon, expressing their delight that Emma was in London and promising to see her that evening at Colhurst House.

At that moment, the door opened and her maid, Milton, entered the room. Draped across her outstretched arms were several shawls, each more beautifully detailed than the last.

"Any of these would look lovely, my lady, but I think the silver one would look the best with your gown."

Emma looked up from the jewel case to assess her reflection in the pier glass. Her deep rose pink gown, with its

deceptively simple empire waist and intricately embroidered puffed sleeves, needed little embellishment.

"Thank you, Milton," she said, turning to the maid, who
was laying the shawls across the bed. "Your taste is impeccable as usual. And the silver shawl has made my choice of
jewelry very easy. I will wear my diamond eardrops and
bracelet."

Milton straightened, her plain face a picture of disappointment. "Is that all, my lady? What about the broach and
necklace?" Milton loved to see her mistress dripping in
jewels.

"No, I believe my gown will show to better advantage
without the distraction of too many baubles."

Milton, long used to expressing her opinion to her mistress, made a face. "The current fashion is for more jewels,
but you always go your own way."

"Yes, I do." Emma sent a smile to her longtime maid before turning her attention back to her image. She assessed
what she saw with critical eyes. Could Milton be right? It
was very important for her to look her best tonight. This
thought caught her up short. Why was tonight different
from any other night? She met her own deep blue eyes in
the glass and saw only confusion.

Tonight was different because Jack Devruex could be at
the ball. There. She finally admitted to herself what she had
been trying to push away since hearing he was in Town.

Closing her eyes, she shut out her too revealing expression. It was getting late, but she couldn't make herself
move away from the mirror.

The evening loomed before her and she felt suspended
between dread and anticipation, all over someone she had
not laid eyes on for thirteen years.

Clenching her hands together, she told herself that she
was being silly. It was highly unlikely that Jack Devruex
would make an appearance at something so tame as Lady
Colhurst's ball. Besides, even if he did, what did it really

matter? Whatever had passed between them had been buried by the passage of so many years.

"My lady? Are you feeling well?"

Milton's concerned tone brought Emma's attention back to the present. Unclenching her fingers, she turned to the worried looking woman.

"Yes, Milton, I am feeling well. Extremely well. Wonderfully well."

Milton picked up the silver shawl and matching reticule. "I'm sure I do not know what that means, my lady, but you had a queer look about you for a moment. I sure wish we could go back home. I don't think Lonun is good for you."

Taking the articles from the frowning maid, Emma smiled affectionately.

"We'll be home soon enough. You will see. The Season will fly by. Now *I* must fly or Grandmère will be cross. No need to wait up for me. I'm sure I'll be quite late."

Milton sniffed. "I've been waiting up for you since your first ball, and I'll be waiting up for you tonight."

Emma ceased adjusting her shawl. *Her first ball.* How strange that Milton would mention that tonight. She had met Jack Devruex at her first ball, and she felt just as nervous tonight as she had then, but for much different reasons.

Taking her wayward nerves well in hand, Emma turned to the stout maid and smiled brightly. "I shall see you in the wee hours then." And with a deep, fortifying breath she swept out of the room.

As the luxurious coach carried them through the narrow streets to Lady Colhurst's townhouse, Emma could feel her grandmother's steely gaze affixed upon her. Pretending to gaze out the window did little to divert the dowager's attention.

A moment later, Emma felt no surprise when Grandmère began to speak in a firm voice.

"I trust that you are done with this wretched teasing

about paramours and other such nonsense. You must be aware that there shall be any number of suitable gentlemen at the ball. You know, my dear, it would be my fondest wish for you to marry again. You are much too young to stay in widow's weeds. This is one of the few things your mother and I agree upon."

Pulling down the canvas blind, Emma suppressed a vexed sigh. Yes, her mother had been hinting for years that she should marry again. Thank goodness Mama had decided to stay in Brighton this spring, for Emma did not think she could bear the both of them haranguing her about marriage.

"Don't you think it's rather odd that neither you nor Mama has married again, yet you both behave as if I must?"

Grandmère clicked her tongue impatiently. "That is not the same thing and you know it. You are much too young and beautiful to remain unmarried."

Emma leaned back against the cushions and felt a mixture of exasperation and amusement. "You were rather young when Grandpapa passed away. You cannot tell me that there were not any number of suitable gentlemen vying for your hand. Kel told me once that even old Noble Rot numbered in their ranks."

"Your brother mistook the connection. The *Marquis of Rottingham*," she emphasized the title with a disapproving sniff at her granddaughter's casual reference to a peer of the realm, "was a very dear and attentive friend."

Emma smiled at this vague explanation. "I never thought to see the day when you, of all people, played coy, Grandmère."

"Bah!" The dowager made a dismissive gesture, the ostrich plumes in her turban aflutter. "Why are you so persistent on this subject? Oh, never mind. I will tell you what you want to hear. Yes, I received a number of flattering offers in my day. So will you, now that you are in London."

Emma lifted her brows. "Why did you not accept any of

those flattering offers?" She kept her tone deliberately mild.

Her grandmother gave a light shrug. "I did not feel the need to marry again."

With a satisfied feeling of triumph, Emma said, "We have much in common, Grandmère, for I too feel no need to marry again."

Even in the dim light of the coach lantern, she could see by her grandmother's slight frown that she was considering her words. Emma thought again how beautiful she was, with her thick white hair, deep blue eyes, and flawless complexion that was the envy of many a younger woman—and a keen intellect to match her beauty.

Emma had always adored her grandmother and never wanted to disappoint her in any way. Yet it pained her to know that on the subject of her possible remarriage, Grandmère was destined to be severely disappointed.

Finally, the dowager began to speak, her tone of voice growing more thoughtful and serious. "I will own that the Wenlock women have always been independent—sometimes to our detriment. After all, who has the power to censure us? You have lived on your own for more than six years and have long been used to making your own decisions. After enduring so many tragedies, first little Henry, then Charles, you have occupied yourself with your school, the orphanage, the farm, and I know not what. I can see that it has been much too long since you have had any amusement. Believe me, my dear, I would be the last person to fault your desire for a, shall we say, flirtation. After all, it is only a natural desire in a young and beautiful woman. But I do know how much Charles hurt you and I would hate to see you get hurt again by being foolish with your heart."

Her grandmother's unexpected words not only touched Emma deeply, but they surprised her too. Grandmère had not mentioned the painful subjects of Henry and Charles in many years. Obviously, her grandmother had given this matter some serious thought. As Emma considered how to respond, the coach trundled up the lane leading to the Colhursts' townhouse. She pushed the blind aside and saw several grooms, torches held aloft, running alongside the carriage to lead it up the drive.

Although she had set out to shock and tease her grandmother last night with her comment about taking a lover, Emma had also wanted to test the waters delicately. Since she was staying with her grandmother for the Season, Emma did not want her to be truly upset if she did decide to embark upon a discreet *affair de coeur*.

However, that particular proposition was a very big *if*.

Despite her bold statement, she was not completely positive that she actually had the nerve to take a lover. Back home, the half-formed notion of engaging in a serious flirtation seemed quite romantic and exciting. Now that she was actually in London, her carefree confidence had wavered.

With resolve, she dismissed thoughts of her romantic future. After all, she had all the lovely Season ahead of her to consider any potential amours. Tonight she would have the wonderful pleasure of dancing at a ball, something she had not done in a very long time.

As the coach rolled to a stop, Emma sent her grandmother a wide smile. "Oh, Grandmère, do not fret over my heart. Truly, there is no need. Besides, Charles did not really hurt me. He could not, for I did not love him."

The old lady looked genuinely shocked. "What? Not ever?"

The door opened and music and laughter spilled from the wide-open doors down to the drive, where a string of coaches was unloading their occupants.

"No, not even a little," she said cheerfully as she followed the dowager from the conveyance.

"My dear Emmaline," Grandmère said with a shake of her head as they took the marble steps up to the crowded entryway, "now I am even more concerned for your heart."

*   *   *

As soon as they made their way to the receiving room that led to the spacious ballroom below, their hostess, Lady Colhurst, greeted the dowager Duchess of Kelbourne and Lady Fallbrook with effusive charm.

As evidenced by the massive and fragrant floral arrangements placed in every corner of the room, the number of footmen circulating among the guests, and the size of the orchestra in the gallery, no expense was too extreme to make Lady Colhurst's ball the most beautiful, welcoming, and exciting of the Season.

As she moved toward the sweeping staircase, an overwhelming array of colors and sounds met Emma's senses. It had been years since she had attended such a large function. Under the pretext of adjusting her shawl, she paused a moment to gain her bearings. Hundreds of guests milled about the ballroom, and their smiling faces, along with the elegant setting, caused her pulse to quicken.

With a dreamy sigh, she turned shining eyes to her grandmother and said, "There really is nothing so congenial as a ball, is there, Grandmère?"

"I have certainly never tired of attending a party arranged by a brilliant hostess," she stated as they began to descend the grand staircase.

Emma could see heads begin to turn toward them as they neared the bottom and she prayed she would not disgrace herself by tumbling down the last few steps.

"Ah, do not be conspicuous by looking, but my old friend Lady Arlington is approaching us and she is with her grandson, Lord Darley," Grandmère said in a low voice as they stepped safely off the landing onto the deeply polished floor. "Now that is what I call a fine figure of a man. He is not only handsome, but imminently suitable."

Smiling at her grandmother's refusal to give up matchmaking, Emma glanced over to see a plump matron in blue accompanied by a handsome blond man making their way toward them.

"Your grace! I was so hoping that we would see you this evening. May I please present my grandson, Lord Darley?"

"How good to see you, Lady Arlington." The dowager's regal smile went from the curtsying lady to her bowing grandson. "And good evening to you, young man. It has been quite some time since I laid my gaze upon you, sir. This is my granddaughter, Lady Fallbrook."

Lord Darley made a most elegant bow over Emma's hand. As he straightened she felt a momentary startlement at the intensity of his warm hazel gaze.

"It is a very great pleasure to make your acquaintance, Lady Fallbrook."

"How kind, sir." Feeling a warm blush rising to her cheeks, Emma could think of nothing else to say. Had she been out of Society for so long that if an attractive gentleman showed his admiration she would blush like a schoolgirl? If she did not take herself in hand she would be in danger of becoming an antidote.

"My dear Lady Fallbrook!" A lilting voice cut through her musings. Emma turned from Lord Darley to see a dark-haired woman dressed in sapphire blue, her gamine face wreathed in smiles, approaching. Emma instantly smiled in response. It was her dear friend Amelia Spence-Jones. "How good to see you, Mrs. Spence-Jones!" They clasped their gloved hands in warm greeting.

"I thought you would never arrive. Oh, good evening, Darley," Amelia said when she noticed Lord Darley at Emma's side. "I did not think we would see you here this evening. I know you will forgive me when I steal Lady Fallbrook from you, for I have not seen my friend in nearly six months. But my dear husband is here. I am sure you will find him in the billiards room." The pretty brunette sent Darley a sweet smile and, without waiting for him to reply, placed her arm through Emma's and drew her away.

Emma could not mistake the look of disappointment that crossed Lord Darley's face. Amused by her friend's enthusiasm, she sent a smile to the handsome man and lifted her shoulders in a helpless gesture. He returned her smile with a broad one of his own and made a sweeping bow.

Perhaps her behavior was not as gauche as she feared, she thought, feeling a measure of her natural confidence returning at his obvious regard.

Emma shifted her gaze to Grandmère, who was still engaged in conversation with Lady Arlington. Catching her eye, Grandmère sent her a quick smile and waved her off with a flutter of her fan.

"My dearest Emmaline!" Amelia said as she squeezed her arm. "Penelope and I have been beyond excited about seeing you this evening. We each promised that whoever saw you first would bring you to the other. Now I have lost sight of her in this mad crush! But we will have the nicest coze while we hunt for her. Oh!" she said, giving Emma's arm another squeeze. "It has been much too long! Your letters are always wonderful, but it is not the same as seeing you."

"Indeed it is not." Emma sent a fond smile to her old friend and was pleased to see how well she looked. Her deep blue gown flattered her striking dark eyes and alabaster complexion. "I am so happy that we shall have the entire spring to visit. I fear you shall grow sick of my company by the end of the Season."

"Impossible! But truly, it is so exciting to have you here. You should hear what everyone is saying about you. No one can speak of anything else. Especially after the scene at Drury Lane last night—what gossip that caused!"

"Dear Amelia, surely you know that I do not care a fig what people say about me," Emma stated as they navigated through the crowd. Despite her dismissive manner, Emma could not deny how amusing she found Amelia's words.

"You do not have to care what others say about you. That's why everyone is so curious to see what you will do next," Amelia said as they sidestepped a clutch of dowagers.

"What I will do next? Heavens, you make me sound like Mrs. Willoughby and her white ponies. There is no reason for anyone to discuss me. I lead an utterly placid life and have done nothing to draw any attention to myself."

Amelia's sudden laughter was a mixture of shock and admiration as she glanced quickly to the other guests crowding around them.

"And that, my dear Lady Emmaline Fallbrook, is why your name is on everyone's lips. The fact that you would even mention Mrs. Wil—well, you know who, at Lady Colhurst's ball when anyone might hear you, is why you are becoming such a rage."

"How silly," Emma said with a shake of her head, hardly believing what her friend said.

"Thank goodness you have come to London," Amelia continued as they walked beneath the gallery where the orchestra was playing a lively reel. "I confess I have been growing quite worried about you over the last year or two."

Amelia's words caught Emma by surprise. "Good heavens! Why?"

"I confess that the last few times I have stayed with you at Maplewood I found the situation most disturbing. All the local mamas were bringing their daughters to you to make their curtsies before their first appearance at the local assembly balls. It was as if you were setting yourself up as some dowager, which was so dreadful, for you are so young and beautiful and used to be so fun-loving."

Emma almost stumbled. "Used to be fun-loving?"

Amelia bit her lip, looking flustered as she struggled to respond.

Suddenly, Emma's expression broke into a smile and her bubbling laughter filled the tense silence. The guests nearest them turned and smiled at the pretty picture the two of them made.

"I'm not offended, dear Amelia. In fact, you are exceedingly observant. My life in Yorkshire has been very useful, very peaceful, and very boring. I have come to London to be young and gay. I think more than six years of respectable widowhood is enough for anyone."

Amelia stopped and looked directly at Emma, a pleased and relieved expression spreading across her pretty features. "Oh, I am so happy to hear this! And you may count on me to help you have lots of fun. You know how my dear husband is so shockingly indulgent and encourages me in all my sprees. We shall set London on its ear with our high spirits. It will not be a challenge, for you are already cutting a dash with your sense of fashion. I just visited my milliner and heard several ladies ordering new bonnets with the 'Fallbrook slant'."

"You are teasing."

"No, I vow it is true. Your uncluttered, elegant style makes the latest mode appear much too fussy. You have been in Town less than a week and already you are considered the best-dressed woman in the beau monde."

"Heavens, what a burden! If I am considered fashionable it is only because I have given my dressmaker her head. I certainly don't care about setting any fashions."

"Well, don't tell anyone—you'll spoil the illusion."

"I had no notion that there was an illusion about me."

"Yes, there is. And you should nurture it. A good illusion keeps everyone fascinated. You are lucky that you don't have to create one. Everyone believes you are the impeccable, unflappable, perfectly perfect Lady Fallbrook."

"Tosh. I am no such thing. And I should hate to be considered so. Being perfectly perfect sounds dreadfully arduous to keep up."

"Of course you are not perfect, but no one needs to know that. Believe me, you will have more fun if you keep up the façade. You know how the *ton* loves the unusual."

"I think you are quite silly, but I have missed you greatly."

"I have missed you too. Now where could Penelope be? This ballroom is not so large that we could completely lose her."

As they moved past a gaggle of twittering misses, Emma was struck by the way they stared at her and whispered to one another behind their fans. Perhaps Amelia's assertions were not so silly after all. Ignoring them, she scanned the guests for her friend.

"At last!" Amelia cried at her side. "We should have guessed that all of the most attractive gentlemen in the room would surround Penelope, though I do not see Lord Tunbridge among them. I would wager that he is in the billiards room with my husband."

With a laugh at Amelia's wry observation, Emma looked over to see her oldest friend holding court in the midst of a group of attentive gentlemen. Emma smiled at the picture Penelope Tunbridge made with her wheat-colored curls and playful smile. They had not seen each other since the autumn and the last letter she had received from Penelope a week ago stated her skepticism that Emma would actually make the journey to London. Emma laughed to herself at how she was about to surprise her old friend.

At that moment, Penelope turned and the look of delight that spread across her heart-shaped face brought a warm glow to Emma's heart.

"Is it really Lady Fallbrook?" she said, reaching for Emma's hands. "So, my dear friend, has our constant haranguing finally compelled you to leave the wilds of Yorkshire and enjoy a little Society?"

Penelope's mossy green eyes were full of mischief and delight as Emma held out her hands in warm greeting. "My dear Lady Tunbridge, I shall confess that you and Mrs. Spence-Jones have been most persuasive. I am delighted to be in London again."

"Wonderful!" The petite beauty turned back to her attentive group of gentlemen. "Oh, you must pardon my rag manners! Lady Fallbrook, have you met Mr. Fitzhugh, Lord Collinwood, and Sir John Mayhew? I know I need not introduce our delightful Mrs. Spence-Jones, for you gentlemen have long been acquainted with her."

After greetings were exchanged with the gentlemen,

Penelope very prettily excused herself and her friends and drew the ladies away.

"I can hardly believe that you are here, Emmaline!" Penelope said once they were several yards away. "I have never seen you in better looks. You must tell me what occurred at the theatre last night, for no one can speak of anything else. My dear Tunbridge—despite how much I praise his patience—has grown positively weary of my rattling on about how excited I am at your arrival," Penelope said, taking a breath, before continuing in her happy, lilting tone. "However, make no mistake, he is very pleased that you have finally come to Town. We are going to have the most splendid dinner party in your honor next week. It is going to be lovely. Amelia expressed her concern that you might have a previous engagement, and I said that if you did, you would just have to cry off, for I shall not easily share you. Besides, there won't be anyone worth spending an evening with who won't be at my house next Tuesday. So there. David and I have several other amusements planned for you, so there will be no nonsense about spending all your time with your grandmother. I know she would not want it anyway, for the duchess is quite busy with her own set. So you see? It is all arranged. We shall have the loveliest time now that you are here."

Emmaline put her hands up in a mock attempt to fend off the onslaught of her friend's words. "Penelope, it is so nice to see you. How is your dear husband? And I trust that your delightful children are well?" she asked with exquisitely dry politeness.

Amelia laughed and Penelope sent them both a sheepish grin. "Oh, you. Forgive me for rattling on, but I have been on pins and needles waiting for you. Freddie and Jane are perfect. My husband is fine. I would hazard a guess that he is in the billiard room with Mr. Spence-Jones. I really am so very glad that you have finally come to Town."

"I am too," Emma said, meeting Penelope's warm gaze with her own.

Suddenly, the opening strains of a waltz filled the air and couples began to pair up and move to the floor.

Emma watched the dancers take their places with great interest. "I have been so long from Society that I confess myself a bit taken aback that Lady Colhurst would permit the waltz. Although I have never seen any real harm in it if the proprieties are observed."

"There is nothing so delightful as a waltz, although some matrons still think it rather fast. I will give Lady Colhurst credit for being extremely modish," Penelope stated, looking around. "Where is my husband? You would think he would be gentlemanly enough to come away from his gaming and dance with me once or twice." Despite her words, Emma suspected that Penelope was not truly vexed at her husband's neglect.

"I am in complete sympathy with you," Amelia said with a doleful shake of her head. "Roger used to be so attentive, but now that we have been married for all of seven years, dancing does not interest him the way it used to."

Over Amelia's shoulder, a familiar figure caught Emma's attention and a smile spread across her features. "Dear Amelia, you are about to cause every married woman the pangs of envy."

Penelope, who saw the same thing Emma did, smiled and nodded her head in agreement.

"Envy? Whatever for?" Amelia looked genuinely perplexed.

"Something most unusual is about to occur—A husband is going to ask his wife to waltz." Although she was teasing the younger woman, Emma felt there was more than a bit of truth in her words.

In the highly sophisticated atmosphere of the *ton,* it was just not done for married couples to live in each other's pockets. But Emma was happy to see, as handsome Roger Spence-Jones wended his way toward his wife through the crowd, that there was at least one couple who obviously did not care about this particular fashion.

A moment later, Roger reached them. "My dear Lady Fallbrook! What a pleasure to see you. I believe it has been close to five months since we stayed with you at Maplewood, which is much too long for my wife to be without your society."

Emma smiled at the handsome man, liking the familiar twinkle in his brown eyes. "Good evening, Mr. Spence-Jones. I confess that it has been much too long."

"As you can judge for yourself, the *ton* is agog with your arrival. And with very good reason."

"It is true," Amelia put in. "We were just discussing how much fun we shall have now that Lady Fallbrook has come to Town."

Penelope sent the gentleman a sly smile. "And I shall count on you to encourage my husband to ignore any scrapes I may get into while Lady Fallbrook is here."

Mr. Spence-Jones laughed. "Of course you may count on me, Lady Tunbridge. But I don't think you will need my assistance, for Tunbridge has always seemed to like your adventures."

"You are too kind," Penelope said with a chuckle.

"Lady Fallbrook, we were very pleased to see your note this morning accepting our invitation to dine tomorrow evening. We shall do our best to amuse you."

"I have no doubt, sir, and I look forward to it."

"Capital! Now, if you will both pardon us, I intend to waltz with my wife." After a bow to Emma and Penelope, he guided Amelia onto the polished floor. Amelia's expression, as she gazed up at her husband, caught at Emma's heart.

Emma stayed still, unable to pull her attention from the look of love and adoration so plainly evident on her friend's pretty face.

As they moved in time to the romantic melody, Emma shifted her gaze to Roger. The expression of passion and protective tenderness stamped on his features caused an odd ache to enter her chest. He did not even attempt to mask his emotions as he gazed down at his wife. Emma continued to watch, transfixed by the charming, shameless intimacy of the two lovers.

Amelia must have said something amusing, for Roger smiled and pulled her a little closer. Her gloved hand caressed his shoulder for a moment. An instant later, Emma lost sight of them amongst the other dancers.

"Aren't they charming?" Penelope said softly at her side.

"Undeniably."

What must it be like to be that in love? Emma wondered, the odd ache still in her heart. What must it be like to have that kind of intimate understanding and devotion? Amelia and Roger were indeed among the most blessed people she knew, for the kind of love they shared, she knew from experience, was very rare indeed.

"Now that is a surprise!" Penelope's words broke into Emma's thoughts and she turned to see the petite blonde gazing toward the entryway. "Lud! If it isn't Lord Monteford! I heard he could not tear himself away from a certain retired actress."

Feeling curious, Emma looked above the heads of the other guests to see the same slim, elegantly handsome man who had been with Mrs. Willoughby at the theatre, coming down the sweeping staircase.

She watched with interest as he descended and joined the throng of guests. He approached their hostess, who by her beaming smile seemed enormously pleased to see him. The flourishing bow he performed was graceful and well practiced.

Although he did not have the engaging good looks of Lord Darley, Viscount Monteford was a handsome man. He looked much as he had last night: formally dressed and exceedingly proud.

She remembered the way he had seemed to enjoy the attention his mistress received at the theatre. She also remembered the impertinent way his eyes had held hers as she had sat in her grandmother's box. What kind of man would flaunt his mistress to half of London, and then practically flirt with another woman at the same time? These kinds of intrigues certainly did not occur back home, she thought with an amused smile.

Just then, Lord Monteford turned from his conversation with Lady Colhurst and looked directly at her. She gazed for a moment into his eyes and felt a blush creeping into her cheeks as a smile slowly came to his lips. He was doing it again! she thought with a flicker of annoyance. As smoothly as she could, she pulled her gaze from his and casually began to scan the room, until she felt a tap on her forearm.

"I would never have thought to see Viscount Monteford here," Penelope continued in a conspiratorial tone. "From everything I have heard, he is quite besotted with a certain jewel of the demimonde and rarely leaves her side. Is it true that at the play last night an actor made some sort of comparison between you and Queen Willow?"

"Yes," Emma said, glancing back to where Lord Monteford stood with their hostess. A look of surprise lurked beneath Lady Colhurst's pleased expression and a number of other guests looked on curiously.

"I thought my grandmother would have a paroxysm when the actor departed from the script."

"I wish I had been there. I saw Mrs. Willoughby"—Penelope lowered her voice on the name—"at the park last week. Quite sets herself up as very superior. I would not be at all surprised if she dubbed herself Queen Willow."

Emma laughed, keeping her gaze on Lord Monteford, who had left their hostess to stand with a group on the other side of the room.

"She did rather behave as if she owned the theatre. I have to say I found her confidence impressive."

"Yes, that is why I am surprised to see Monteford here tonight. But seeing him puts me in mind of his friend."

Emma caught Penelope's serious gaze as she continued. "I have to ask if you are aware that Lord Devruex is in Town."

Although Emma was surprised to hear that Lord Monteford and Jack Devruex were acquainted, she had prepared herself for Penelope's question. She was quite proud of herself when she did not become flustered.

It was only natural that Penelope would be concerned about her encountering Jack Devruex, for she was one of the few people who knew the true details of what happened all those years ago.

"Yes, I heard last night. It's not really surprising, is it?"

"No. My husband is quite impressed with Devruex's stables and says he is becoming quite the star in the racing world."

Instantly, the memory of a young Jack Devruex telling her of his dreams and plans for breeding thoroughbreds washed over her in a stinging wave. His eloquent enthusiasm had captured her young imagination and there had been a time when nothing seemed more exciting to her than helping him build his stable.

So he had achieved some of his goals, she thought with grudging admiration. Briefly, she wondered where he had gotten the capital to start his venture.

"Good evening again, Lady Fallbrook," a voice reached her above the music and broke into her thoughts. Emma turned around and met a pair of smiling hazel eyes.

"Lord Darley!" she said warmly, glad she remembered his name after their brief introduction earlier.

"I confess that I have been trying to reach you for the last half an hour. I almost believed I was destined to chase you from one end of the ballroom to the other."

Before she could stop it, surprised laughter escaped her lips as she met his admiring gaze.

"I certainly had no notion that I was being chased, but I will not apologize for unknowingly evading you in case you needed the exercise." Emma thought him quite charming as well as handsome as he laughed at her rejoinder. "Are you acquainted with Lady Tunbridge, sir?"

At Emma's question, Penelope sent Lord Darley a wide smile and answered for him. "Lud, yes. How are you, Darley? I spoke to your mother a while ago. She looks very well."

"She is, thank you. I do not have to ask after your health, Lady Tunbridge, for you grow lovelier every time we meet."

"You are such a charmer, sir." Just then a woman in a flamboyant yellow gown approached and drew Penelope's attention away.

Lord Darley grinned at Emma and made a sweeping gesture toward the dancers. "I noticed that you have not yet danced. May I have the honor of being the first to lead you onto the floor this evening?"

Her smile broadened and she owned that she felt flattered by the admiration so evident in his smiling eyes.

With Penelope in conversation with her friend, Darley led Emma to the other dancers. Taking a deep breath, she did her best to relax, but her nerves felt rather racked for she had only ever waltzed with her brother and uncle—and that had been during private family gatherings.

A moment later, as his warm hand rested upon her waist, it became apparent that she needn't have been nervous, for Lord Darley proved to be an excellent dancer.

It felt wonderful to be whirled around the floor in time to beautiful, lilting music. And she found it even more gratifying that he also showed every evidence of enjoying himself. Charles had hated dancing. Instantly, she dismissed thoughts of her deceased husband, for she wanted nothing unpleasant to intrude upon this lovely evening.

Lord Darley skillfully led her around the floor and Emma relaxed even more, finding him extremely easy to follow. Oh, she had missed this! It had been too many years since she had experienced this heady feeling of dancing in

the arms of a handsome, attentive man. This moment alone
made the trip to London well worth it.

"Shall you be staying for the entire Season, Lady Fallbrook?"

"Yes. Even so, I don't know how there will be enough
time to attend all the parties and other entertainments that
my grandmother has planned."

"I shall have to pay the duchess my highest compliments
for convincing you to spend the Season in Town."

"And she will certainly take all the credit," Emma said
with wry humor as he swung her into a graceful turn.

"Lady Fallbrook, would you do me the honor of accom-
panying me on a drive through Hyde Park tomorrow afternoon?"

A pang of disappointment brought a slight frown to her
brow. "I'm sorry Lord Darley, but I am to spend tomorrow
afternoon shopping with my grandmother."

For a moment he looked crestfallen, and then said, "I
shall be devastated if you say you are engaged the day after
tomorrow."

She felt charmed by his earnestness. "I am not, sir. I
would enjoy driving in the park with you on Thursday."

With the melodic strains of music and the excited chatter of the other guests swirling around them, Emma gazed
into his eyes and came to a momentous decision.

Lord Darley certainly exhibited all the traits she was
looking for in a gentleman. He possessed engaging, easy
manners and had a wonderful sense of humor. He was an
excellent dancer and her grandmother certainly found him
acceptable. Yes, Lord Darley was certainly a gentleman
worthy of being the first name on her list of potential
lovers. Not that she intended to make any snap decisions
this early in the Season, but he was certainly attractive
enough to give further consideration.

A ripple of excitement raced over her skin at her own
daring.

The music faded away and they came to a stop. Emma

was the first to lower her gaze from the intensity of Lord Darley's.

They remained silent as he began to lead her through the densely packed dance floor back to where Penelope now stood with Grandmère and a number of her friends, as well as Amelia and Roger.

The look of approval and pleasure so plainly evident on Grandmère's countenance almost made Emma laugh. The old lady would be calling for the banns to be read after one waltz, Emma thought with rueful amusement.

She moved to stand next to Grandmère, then turned back to Lord Darley. "Thank you, sir, for a lovely dance."

"The pleasure is mine, my lady." With another lingering look, Lord Darley bowed and left.

Just as Emma turned to tease her grandmother over her too pleased expression, their hostess caught her attention. Although some distance away she was looking directly at Emma.

The plump lady—dyed orange egret feathers quivering atop her head—moved gracefully, yet swiftly, through the crowd with a pleased smile gracing her features.

As Lady Colhurst drew near, Emma noticed the man at her side. She was startled to see that it was Lord Monteford.

"La, Emmaline, it appears Monteford desires to judge for himself if what the actor said last night about your charms is true," Penelope whispered to her from behind her fan.

Their hostess and Lord Monteford were now so close that Emma dared not risk replying to Penelope.

"My dear Lady Fallbrook," Lady Colhurst said without preamble, "what a delightful picture you made waltzing with Lord Darley. I trust you will delight us by taking the floor again." This last bit was said with a bright sideways smile to the gentleman at her side. "Now then, I do not believe you know Lord Monteford."

Keenly aware of her grandmother's and her friends' interested attention, Emma composed her features into a faint smile and said, "No, Lady Colhurst, I have not had the pleasure of meeting Lord Monteford. Good evening, sir."

Inclining her head toward him, she watched his smile disappear and his brows furrow ever so slightly. For an instant she feared that her tone had been a bit too frosty, and then decided she did not care. By the avid stares from a number of the other guests, it was clear that most of them had heard about the scene at the theatre last night. Well, she was in no humor to provide more gossip for the scandal-mongering appetite of the *ton*.

She held his gaze steadily for a moment and was suddenly struck by the unusual color of his eyes. Last night, in the indifferent light of the theatre, she would not have suspected their startling beauty. They were a dark, flawless blue, like a perfect sapphire.

He held his chin high before he made a bow to Grand-mère and the rest of the group. It looked as if he was about to speak when Grandmère snapped her fan open and said, "So how is your mother, young man? Last time I called upon her, I was distressed to see that she had taken to her hartshorn for some inexplicable reason."

Emma bit her lip to hide her amusement. How like her grandmother to make a not so subtle reference to the common knowledge that Monteford's mama was distraught over his scandalous behavior with his mistress.

By Lord Monteford's calm expression, it appeared he was completely unperturbed by the dowager's jibe. "Thank you for your concern, Duchess. My mother has always been fragile, but she never misses her Tuesday evening whist party, which I believe you attend as well, ma'am?"

Grandmère sent him a brittle smile. "I do indeed. We always enjoy the *liveliest* conversation." Again, there seemed to be another level of meaning to the old lady's words.

Lord Monteford's lips compressed, but he obviously thought better of sparring any more with the dowager Duchess of Kelbourne.

"Lady Fallbrook, Lady Colhurst informs me that the

next set will be a quadrille. I would be honored if you would dance with me."

The quadrille! That elegant dance had always been a particular favorite of Emma's. Something about moving in harmonious synchronicity with the other dancers, weaving the figures in graceful time with the music, had always had an almost mesmerizing effect upon her senses. As a girl, when she had first learned the complicated steps, she had fancied that if the dancers carried long ribbons, by the end of the dance they would all be entwined in an intricate braid.

"I would be delighted, Lord Monteford."

He offered his arm and she placed her fingers on his forearm, then sent a smile to her grandmother. The old lady did not look as pleased as she had when Emma had taken the floor with Lord Darley.

Doing her best to ignore the stares from the other guests, Emma moved to stand opposite Lord Monteford and waited for the other dancers to take their places.

Glancing around the room, she noticed Penelope joining another set with her husband. Evidently, Lord Tunbridge decided to leave the billiard room after all, she thought with a smile. She continued to watch as Penelope leaned toward her husband and pointed to Emma. The earl turned with a broad smile and sent Emma a jaunty salute just as the music started. She smiled back at her friend's handsome husband, glad that there were a few familiar faces among the hundreds crowding the ballroom.

She and Lord Monteford danced in silence for a few measures, and Emma noticed that although the quadrille was a completely different kind of dance compared to the waltz, he did not possess Lord Darley's easy grace. Oh, he performed the steps well enough, but his manner was a little too studied to be truly pleasing, Emma decided.

She hoped he was not the kind of gentleman who talked through the whole dance. For the quadrille in particular she preferred little or no conversation. Jack had always re-

mained silent when they had danced together. She recalled
the way his intense dark eyes held hers as they formed the
figures. It had been dizzyingly romantic to gaze into his
eyes as the room swirled around them.

With a jolt of shock, she realized that she was actually
remembering something about Jack Devruex with fondness. Forcing her disturbing thoughts back to the present,
she sent Lord Monteford a bright smile.

"Did you enjoy the play last night, Lady Fallbrook?" he
asked in a silky voice.

For an instant, she lost the rhythm of the music and
made the *chasse* a second too slow. She studied his haughty
features for a moment, wondering what he was about. She
certainly did not intend to comment on the impudent actor's
bizarre departure from the play. "I thought the perform-
ances rather amateurish." She kept her tone deliberately
light.

Monteford crossed in front of her, making conversation
impossible for a few measures. When they met again in the
center, he wore a slight smile. "Is that all, Lady Fallbrook?
There were a few moments when I would have sworn that
you were enjoying yourself."

He was an intriguing man, she thought as they made the
demi-prominade. If he intended to impress her, making
veiled references to his public appearance with his mistress
was not the way to go about it. "The evening held a few di-
versions," she said.

Not that she cared about Lord Monteford's behavior, but
even her departed husband, a man with a complete want of
sensitivity, had taken pains to be discreet about his affairs.

Passing behind Lord Monteford, she concentrated on the
steps for a few moments. Again they met in the middle,
clasped hands, and spun around in place. He looked deeply
into her eyes and she found something compelling in their
unexpectedly beautiful depths.

"You are an astoundingly fine-looking woman," he murmured softly, "and I have every intention of furthering our acquaintance."

As he released her, Emma's brows shot up. His tone was so confident, so definite, that she could not resist the immediate desire to take the wind out of his sails. Besides, she was not a woman to tolerate being flirted with by a man who flaunted his mistress without a hint of shame.

Sending him a dry look, she said, "Gracious me, Lord Monteford, I would not have thought that you would have the time."

He watched her for a moment, his gaze sharp and assessing. "I have time for all the things that interest me."

Emma decided that notwithstanding his exceedingly pretty eyes and impressive address, she would not be adding the viscount to her list of potential paramours. Being among the "things that interest him" held no attraction for her.

The set ended a moment later and Lord Monteford led her back to her grandmother. Spreading open her fan, Emma turned to him with a cool smile. "Thank you for a most pleasant interlude, sir."

His fair brows rose and Emma could see his barely concealed displeasure. Evidently Lord Monteford was unused to being dismissed. He briefly bowed over her hand, and as he straightened, he looked into her eyes with unconcealed annoyance and confusion. Without a word, he turned and melded into the crowd.

With a dismissive shrug, Emma watched Lord Monteford's retreating back before turning to her grandmother and friends. Grandmère gazed at her with an expression of pride and pleasure.

"Considering the attention you are receiving, you comport yourself exceedingly well, m'dear," Grandmère murmured in a tone the others could not hear. "No one would suspect that you have spent the last decade rusticating. Well done, my dear. You are certainly my granddaughter," she murmured on a note of pride.

"You no longer think I am so provincial?" Emma sent her a rueful smile.

"Certain instincts may have gotten rusty, but you never forget. Are you enjoying yourself?"

"Actually, I am," Emma replied. And she meant it.

But Grandmère's point was not lost upon her. Emma could not help but be keenly aware of the interested stares and whispers directed toward her. She found it rather disconcerting and was grateful for the company of her friends to give her confidence a bit of a boost. She had forgotten how exhausting Society could be.

"I say, look who just walked in. Lady Colhurst is going to be utterly puffed up with pride," Amelia Spence-Jones, standing on the other side of Grandmère, announced.

At the amusement lacing her friend's voice, Emma glanced around, curious as to what elicited the comment. As if drawn by some unseen power, her gaze instantly went to the other side of the room to where a tall man with black hair and broad shoulders was about to descend the curving staircase.

Feeling the air seem to freeze in her lungs, Emma stared. He paused on the landing, his legs braced slightly apart, surveying the scene below.

Jack, Baron Devruex, had just entered the ballroom.

Chapter Four

Upon entering Colhurst House, Jack asked himself for the hundredth time why he had decided to subject himself to what would no doubt be an utterly dull evening. The thought of spending hours dancing with inquisitive matrons and giggling misses almost made him turn on his heel and head to the nearest alehouse. Yet here he was.

Handing his hat and walking stick to a footman, he made his way through the densely packed reception rooms toward the ballroom. To give Lady Colhurst her due, she did go to extravagant lengths to provide her male guests commodious accommodations for cards and billiards. But a pleasant card room had never been enough inducement to bring him to this kind of crush. Yet here he was, he thought again.

There was no point in lying to himself, he thought with grim amusement. He had come to have a look at Lady Fallbrook. At the top of the staircase, the bewigged major domo bowed and stepped forward to announce him to the assemblage.

Jack raised his hand in a brief motion and the major domo instantly halted his movement and sent the baron a look of questioning surprise.

"No need to announce me, good man. Everyone will know I am here soon enough."

At this unprecedented departure from protocol, a grin

flashed across the servant's features before he bowed again, saying placidly, "Very good, milord."

As Jack descended the staircase, his gaze swept the crowd. Not surprisingly, the cream of the beau monde was in attendance. Everyone knew that Lady Colhurst was a notorious stickler when it came to her guest list. Only the most unblemished reputations made it through her door, making her invitation all the more coveted.

Jack knew well enough that the only reason he was welcomed into this hallowed room was that Lady Colhurst had been one of his mother's dearest friends. In her memory, Lady Colhurst graciously ignored his reputation and sent him invitations to every party she hosted during the Season. He had long suspected that the good lady believed that she could reform him with her motherly concern. So far, her efforts had not produced satisfactory results.

In the guise of looking for his hostess, he continued scanning the assemblage, wondering if he would recognize Emma after thirteen years. He saw any number of friends and acquaintances, but was caught up short when he saw Monteford standing by a set of French doors with a group of dandies. Jack was surprised to see him, for he knew the viscount found this kind of affair even more objectionable than he did.

Of course, he mused cynically, it did not surprise him that Monteford had received an invitation from the fastidious Lady Colhurst. Despite the fact that Monteford's reputation was as derelict as Devruex's, Monteford enjoyed the benefit of being shielded from public censure by the power and prestige of his grandfather, the Earl of Pellerton.

A moment later he mentally dismissed his friend, deciding to speak to him later. Right now his sole focus was on locating Lady Fallbrook.

He scanned the room for all of three seconds before he found her. For a moment, it was as if the more than four hundred guests disappeared.

She stood directly beneath a low slung, massive chandelier. Her shimmering rose-colored gown echoed the glow in the high planes of her cheeks. Her light brown hair, piled high upon her head, showed to advantage the exquisite length of her neck.

Everything about her face and form struck him at once as utterly familiar and completely strange. Gone was the laughing, beautiful girl he'd adored, and in her place stood a strikingly lovely and sophisticated woman. Her figure, although a bit slimmer than he remembered, still had the lush curves that had nearly driven him insane when he had been a besotted one-and-twenty-year-old. My God, had thirteen years really gone by? He could not tell it by the beautiful woman standing on the other side of the ballroom.

He stayed motionless for a moment, feeling the air constrict in his lungs, watching her speak to the dowager Duchess of Kelbourne. Just then, he caught sight of a smiling Lady Colhurst approaching. With an effort, he pulled himself from his near frozen contemplation of Emmaline Fallbrook and moved to bow over his hostess's proffered hand.

"My dear Lord Devruex, I cannot tell you how delighted I am to see you this evening! I can hear hearts fluttering all over the room as we speak. Oh, I am not precipitous when I say that my ball is an unequivocal success. Now you will never guess who else has joined us this evening," she said. Putting her arm through his, she drew him farther into the room as she continued to chatter.

Only half listening to Lady Colhurst relay the latest *on dit,* Devruex kept his peripheral attention on Emmaline.

It was rather the damnedest thing, he thought, but now that he was here, he had no real plan as to how to proceed. Earlier, he had told himself that he only wanted to take a look at her. After all, the whole Town was talking of nothing else and his curiosity was piqued. Considering what had occurred between them, who would blame him? But now that he had seen her, he had no idea what he intended to do next.

He continued to escort his prattling hostess around the room, hating this uncharacteristically indecisive feeling.

One would think that he had not spent the last thirteen years making crucial decisions about his life. He had gambled his past and risked his future, and through it all he had rarely hesitated or made a misstep. But tonight he could not even decide if he wanted to walk across the room and bow to a woman he had not seen in thirteen years. Gad, it was not as if she still had the power to rip his heart out and leave it on the side of a muddy road again, he thought with bitter humor.

"Now, young man"—Lady Colhurst cut into his thoughts, giving his forearm a firm squeeze—"I expect you shall want to please me by partnering as many ladies as possible this evening," she instructed with a bright smile before turning to her other guests.

Lady Colhurst left him standing in the midst of the festive crowd and his gaze instantly returned to Emmaline. Her profile reminded him again of the first night they met at Lady Cowper's ball, and his heart began to pound with irritating intensity.

Enough of this hesitation, he thought impatiently as he moved toward her through the densely packed ballroom. This meeting was long past due.

Deliberately ignoring anyone who tried to gain his attention, he kept his gaze on Emmaline's graceful form.

Had the time come to forgive her? The thought caught him up short. What a strange notion to enter his mind at this moment. Feeling his hands clench into fists, he slowed his stride to give himself some time.

He reminded himself of the enormous risks he had taken to create the life he now lived. He'd staked sums of hard-won capital, the loss of which could have sent him into utter ruin and penury. In light of what had transpired in the last thirteen years, crossing the room to say good evening to Lady Fallbrook should be a mere trifle. Yet, to his continuing annoyance, it was not.

Just then, she turned from the Countess of Tunbridge and looked directly into his eyes. Her lovely face was serene, unreadable. Her cool sea blue gaze passed over him without so much as a flicker of recognition.

He stopped for an instant as an unexpected wave of cold anger gripped his insides. Taking a deep breath, he fought for calm as the memory of the last time he saw her came back with such clarity he remained where he stood, uncaring of the attention he drew to himself.

Thirteen years ago
The Vale of Kelbourne, Kent

On a rise, far above a night-shrouded valley, Kelbourne Keep loomed before him like some gargantuan dragon slumbering in the gleaming moonlight. He turned his gaze away from the imposing castle as he pulled on the reins to slow his trotting cattle.

The lane he traveled upon, though dark and lonely, held few surprises as he tooled his carriage around ruts toward the designated tree, the one with the gnarled scar from a long-ago lightning strike. He breathed in the balmy night air and murmured reassuringly to his skittish horses.

He glanced up again, and saw the impressive dwelling through the rising bank of trees and wondered if Emma had managed to get away from the place yet. He did not need to consult his fob watch to know that it was well past midnight, for when he had left the Bell and Candle some time ago, the clock in the common room read half past eleven.

A misting rain began to fall and he pulled the silver flask from his coat and took another quaff of the biting liquid.

It still seemed almost inconceivable that the incomparable Lady Emmaline Wenlock was about to run away with him. *No, it is not inconceivable. We belong together,* he told himself fiercely, lifting the flask to his lips once more.

Stuffing the flask back in his pocket, he again looked at the massive structure looming in the distance. He reminded himself, and not for the first time, that his name was as good the Kelbournes'. The barony of Devruex was actually older than the Kelbourne dukedom. The first Devruex had come over with William the Conqueror. He had served William bravely and faithfully and the king had bestowed upon him the barony as well as his beautiful cousin's hand in marriage. It had been instilled in Jack from birth that there were few families in England who had more reason to be proud of their lineage than the Devruexs.

That is, until his father had taken the name and made it a byword for disgrace.

He flexed his fingers around the ribbons and spoke to his uneasy cattle. But his thoughts would not let him have any peace regarding the action he and Emma were about to take.

If only her uncle had not refused him, they would not be forced to such drastic measures.

Reaching into his pocket for the flask, he cursed his father for selling almost everything that represented the history of the Devruexs, all to feed his irresistible need to gamble. No doubt if Kingsmount had not been entailed, his father would have sold it as well.

Taking a deep breath, he forced the bitter thoughts from his mind. Tonight, none of that mattered.

Emmaline, Emmaline, Emmaline. His heart sang her name and his chest tightened as he tried to see down the moon-shadowed lane, willing her to appear. He knew he could not relax until they were together. His horses must have sensed his mood, for they neighed and tossed their heads restively.

Raising his gaze to the sky, he saw fingers of heavy clouds spreading across the face of the full moon. He cursed under his breath. He was depending on the moonlight to guide him out of this remote country.

Nevertheless, he refused to allow the threatening weather to dampen his excitement. Any moment she would find him and they would head for the border. Once they were married it wouldn't matter what anyone else thought or said.

Once they were married. The thought of the threadbare draperies and carpets awaiting them at Kingsmount made him reach for his flask again. It pierced his pride to think of her living in the wreck of his home.

Tonight, that did not matter either. The only thing that did matter was that she would be here any moment and they would be flying through the night toward their future.

Nothing else mattered except that his life would start anew because everything that gave it purpose and joy would be at his side.

He continued to wait beneath the gnarled tree, feeling an uncharacteristic sense of patience settle over him. Everything would be fine. It had to be.

When he fumbled returning the flask to his pocket, it occurred to him that he had eaten little since breakfast. After the several draws from his flask, on top of the tankard of ale he had drunk at the posting inn, he'd probably consumed enough false courage for one night, he thought with a wry laugh.

Besides, he did not need courage for everything was going as planned, he reminded himself.

From the moment they had been introduced two and a half months ago, every other interest and pursuit faded before this sudden and single-minded desire to be with Lady Emmaline Wenlock.

Of course, like everyone else, he had heard that the announcement of her engagement to Charles Fallbrook was imminent. But those rumors had not caused him even a moment's pause.

Charles Fallbrook was not his only rival for Emmaline. Every other eligible buck in Town was smitten by Lady Emma. Not only was she unusually beautiful, but she was also quick witted and up for any spree. Her sparkling personality had captured the beau monde, and within a week of her arrival in Town, Beau Brummel himself had declared her an Incomparable.

Spooked by the caw of some night bird, the horses neighed and fidgeted, but Jack's thoughts never left Emma.

His love for her had been so immediate and intense that, from their first dance, he had had to resist the urge to take her by the hand, walk out of the ballroom, and hang the scandal.

Despite his straitened circumstances, Jack felt confident about his future. After all, his father had not been able to sell off everything the Devruexs had accumulated over the centuries, and he was—thankfully—no longer able to accrue any more debt.

Jack's pride had prevented him from revealing to Emma that since his father's death more than a year ago, he had been reeling from the discovery of how bad his father's gambling excesses really were.

It was shameful enough to owe tradesmen such enormous sums, but to find out that his father had left debts of honor had been the most lowering news of all.

The day he had discovered the sheet of parchment in his father's desk, with its neatly written columns of gambling losses, had been the darkest day of his life. His father had lost staggering sums of blunt to some of the most prominent men in the realm.

Feeling the sting of mortification with every quill stroke, Jack had immediately sent letters to all the gentlemen, simply explaining his circumstances and promising to settle the debts as soon as he was able.

To his surprise, most of the peers had written back, expressing the very generous desire that the new baron dismiss the matter completely.

Jack's relief that he would not have to immediately sell more family heirlooms was matched by his determination to pay back every guinea and remove the stain from his name.

But his relief was short-lived, for one of the gentlemen

who had been so gracious about the gambling debt turned out to be none other than Emma's uncle and guardian, Lord Chilcrest.

Jack took another swig from the flask as he recalled the day he approached Lord Chilcrest about marrying Emma. The gentleman had not been as gracious about this matter.

Lord Chilcrest had made it exceedingly clear that it was one thing to forgive the debt of a deceased peer and quite another thing to give his consent for his niece—one of the greatest heiresses in the land—to wed a penniless, disreputable young man.

"It matters not that your family name was once respected," Lord Chilcrest had stated coldly. "Lady Emmaline was made for much greater things." He rose from his chair, an indication that Jack should take his leave.

But Jack had not been so easily dismissed. He refused to walk out before being heard and continued to earnestly press his case. He tried to explain about his plans to refurbish his farms and start a thoroughbred stable.

But the cold-eyed gentleman had not been moved. "You are overreaching yourself, sir" was how he concluded the interview.

Jack had left Lord Chilcrest's townhouse feeling frustrated and embarrassed, but undeterred. As long as Emmaline loved him, nothing could prevent him from marrying her.

The encounter with Emma's uncle had taken place the day before yesterday. To his utter relief and joy, Emma had been just as determined to be with him as he was with her. The last thirty-six hours had been a whirlwind of planning and preparing. He and Emma had worked out a simple scheme to flee to Scotland to be married.

She had left London on the pretext that she was too distraught to stay for the rest of the Season and headed for Kelbourne Keep, the family's country seat. None of her other family members were in residence, so they knew their plan could not fail.

Once they were married, they would face the wrath of her family together. No matter how powerful her relations were, he would not allow them to abuse her. As he sat in his carriage on the dark and lonely lane, he vowed that he would love and protect Lady Emmaline Wenlock for the rest of his life.

Exactly how he would do this without any blunt was a question that made him reach for his flask again.

"I am here, Jack."

He jumped at the softly spoken words and it took a moment to control the surging horses. As soon as he did, he set the brake and leapt from the conveyance and swept her into his arms in a fierce embrace. It was not until his lips were on hers that he realized that the misting rain had turned into a heavy shower.

"Emma, Emma, Emma," he murmured against her soft, warm cheek as he felt her arms tighten around his neck. A moment later, he pulled back to look at her beautiful face.

Her eyes, black pools in the moonlight, held his gaze. Her lips were slightly parted and there was a look of concern mingling with pleasure on her perfect oval features. "Are you all right, Jack?" she asked a little breathlessly.

"Never more now that you are here."

They held each other again, unheeding of the rain, even though her pelisse was already soaked.

"I love you so much," she said. "I was almost afraid that you would not be here."

He laughed. "I will always be here, dearest Emma. Now are you ready to head for Scotland?"

"Yes, please." Her laugh of delight matched his.

Releasing her, he glanced down and saw her portmanteau. Reaching down, he picked it up, moved to the back of the carriage, and unbuckled the wide leather straps in preparation to secure the case. "Did you have any trouble leaving the keep?"

"No, I was only a little nervous in case one of the servants saw me," she said, wiping the rain from her cheeks.

She walked around to join him. "Jack, do not you think that a phaeton—a high-perch phaeton—might be a bit conspicuous for our purpose? We shall be traveling for days, at least, and an open carriage seems foolhardy."

In the silver gloom of the night, he could see her furrowed brow, and the slightly tremulous tone made him abandon his task to pull her into a loose embrace. "I did not have time to arrange for another carriage. But we will be fine."

She looked doubtful. Even though he had been honest with her about his straitened circumstances, it probably never occurred to her that he would not own another conveyance. Because her life had been one of unfettered wealth and privilege, she could not truly know what it was like to struggle. He just counted himself lucky that his father had deemed the phaeton too fashionable to sell, or he would not have any kind of conveyance at all.

"It seems to me this will be a difficult vehicle to handle on a cross-country trip. And it's raining. . . ." The tremor in her tone increased.

Putting his hands up to cup her wet cheeks, he said, "Do not worry, my love. We shall be safe. I will never allow your family to frighten you again."

Even in the indifferent light, he could see the confusion cross her features. "Frighten me? Whatever are you speaking of?" The confusion turned to suspicion. "How much have you been drinking?"

"Just a bit," he said with a grin. "Now shall we go?"

She stared at him for a moment, her expression still confused and a little scared. He stayed motionless, waiting for her answer, suddenly unsure of himself. He did not understand what had occurred to make her suddenly skittish.

Finally, to his immense relief, she nodded, albeit a little hesitantly. Without a word, he helped her up onto the seat. After leaping up beside her, he released the brake and with a flick of the ribbons the horses set off at a fast trot.

They drove, as the rain continued to soak them, in silence for some time before he became aware that Emma was behaving strangely. He glanced over to see her staring at him, her hands gripping the edge of the seat. Frowning, he was about to question her when she suddenly spoke sharply.

"Stop, Jack! Stop at once!"

Yanking back on the reins, the horses kicked up mud as they skidded to a stop. An instant later, she had jumped down from the rocking phaeton and stood on the shadowed road staring up at him.

Her look of shattered disappointment caused his heart to lurch in alarm. "What are you doing? If we don't hurry someone may become aware that you are missing and raise an alarm before we reach the border."

Even in the dim silver glow of the moonlight he could see the tears pooling in her eyes. Her half-sad, half-hysterical laugh caused the horses to start nervously.

"Reach the border! We are in Kent, for Heaven's sake! An alarm will be raised before we are out of the county."

As he opened his mouth to reassure her, she threw her hands up in a despairing gesture. "You are so foxed that you have not even noticed you've been driving in the wrong direction for the last three miles." Lowering her head, she covered her face with her hands.

Peering down the dark road in surprise, he felt a hot flush come to his face at his stupid mistake. Feeling a little fuzzy, he struggled for something to say to calm her down and get her back in the carriage.

"Emma, I—"

"Have I been a fool?"

The muffled, anguished words had him scrambling down from the carriage. Swiftly moving to her, he put his hands on her arms, feeling his feet sinking slightly in the muddy lane. "Emma, I love you more than anything. Please don't worry. There is nothing to be afraid of."

She did not move, and his heart felt as if it were choking him. "We will make up the time," he continued a little desperately. "I have mapped out a way to take less traveled roads—they will not find us, I promise."

Finally, she raised her head and looked up at him. He saw anger beneath the crushed look of disappointment. "Can you know so little about my relationship with my family? I have no reason to be afraid of them. They only want the best for me. Do you have no notion of what it means to be the daughter of a duke, the sister of a duke? I have defied my mother, my grandmother, and my uncles to run away with you. I entrusted myself to you at the risk of being utterly ruined. The people who love me would be shocked, shamed, and disappointed by the action I was about to take."

At the word *was* he instantly realized how close he was to losing her and a sick feeling washed over him. He cast about for something to say to put everything right. From the beginning he had always been able to tease her into a laugh. Recklessly, he attempted light humor now. "Come, my love, just point me in the right direction and let's be gone. You can tease me about this later."

With a jerk, she pulled away from him. "I was willing to give you everything and yet you come to me like this—half foxed and lost. How could you treat this decision as if it were a lark? I trusted you with everything that I am. I can now see that I have been a fool. Good-bye, Jack."

And with that last choked whisper she had turned back toward Kelbourne Keep, leaving him and his heart in the mud.

Chapter Five

*H*is hair is just as black as I remembered. This odd thought was the first thing that registered on Emma's confounded senses. Why should it not be? He was barely four and thirty, she reminded herself distractedly.

But there were a few things that had changed, she noted, her eyes sweeping over him as he descended the stairs with graceful athleticism. Gone was the rangy frame she had found so endearing. His broad-shouldered, muscular frame appeared seasoned and well honed. His thighs, bulging at each step, evidenced long hours in the saddle.

As he reached the floor, he smiled down at their hostess, who appeared delighted by his arrival. Even from this distance Emma could see that the dimples she had adored were deeper and there was a hint of very attractive crinkles around his eyes. His eyes—she recalled them with a shiver, wondering if they were as black and full of mischief as they had been all those years ago.

His nose, longish and straight as a razor, was also just as she remembered. His pale skin, angled cheekbones, and square jaw line were arranged in the same devastatingly masculine fashion that had caused her young heart to race erratically when she had met him at her first London ball.

The cheerful hum of voices quieted for a moment. She saw most of the ladies watching him, but he did not take notice and spoke to their hostess as if she were the only woman in the room. Well, that trait had not changed, she thought wryly.

Just then, she saw his dark head turn and suddenly she was gazing directly into eyes as black as his evening coat. He moved away from Lady Colhurst and began striding toward her through the crowded room.

A maelstrom of indescribable emotions swirled through her body as her heart started thudding in a painfully rapid rhythm.

There could be no mistaking his intention. He was coming straight for her.

The guests milling between them furled back like the petals of a rose. Within seconds, if he did not veer from his present course, he would reach her.

In a way, a part of her felt no surprise at seeing him. From the beginning of the evening she had been aware of a certain tension permeating the very air. Now her overwrought mood almost felt like some sort of presentiment. It seemed clear that after thirteen years the stars had finally aligned in the proper order to bring them to this moment.

As she gripped her fan until her fingers hurt, the voices of the chattering guests became distant and indistinguishable. Glancing up at the chandelier, she hesitated as the thousands of candle flames became hazy orange halos.

Once, many years ago, she had fainted. It had felt just like this then, before everything had gone black and she had fallen to the floor. Damnation, she thought, as the candle glow faded into distant pinpoints of lights.

As suddenly, and as welcome, as a touch from an angel, Emma felt Penelope's cool hand grip her arm and steady her.

Emma took a deep, shuddering breath. She hadn't fainted, and now that the initial wave of panic had thankfully receded, her head began to clear and the room righted itself. Sending her friend a slight smile, Emma straightened her shoulders.

This was not so terrible, she told herself, grasping the thought with all the desperation of a drowning woman. The sense of unreality that had gripped her for the last few moments vanished. Jack Devruex was here. For the first time in thirteen years, she was in the same room as the man who had utterly broken her heart and changed her life.

She lifted her chin, feeling her natural confidence begin to return. Yes, she had coped with far worse than Lord Devruex. Let him come.

An instant later, he stood before her and her friends, bowing. "Lord Devruex!" Grandmère said, and Emma was surprised by the pleasure in the old lady's tone. "What a delight to see you this evening."

"The delight is all mine, Duchess," he said, lifting the hand Grandmère proffered to his lips.

Emma suppressed a shiver as his voice rumbled over her. The tone was deeper and richer than she remembered. He greeted everyone else and it was apparent by their response that he was acquainted with all of her friends.

He certainly had filled out, she observed with a sense of unreality. Even in the elegance of his evening clothes, his muscular frame seemed a little too menacing for this refined company.

"Lady Fallbrook," Grandmère said with exquisite politeness. "I'd like to present Lord Devruex. I believe the two of you may have known each other years ago. Devruex's dear grandparents were very good friends of mine."

He bowed before Emma, and as he rose, her eyes met his. They were just as full of devilment as when they had met so long ago, also, ironically, in a crowded ballroom. Yet the regard and admiration she remembered were conspicuously gone.

Emma inclined her head, unable to find her voice. Summoning all her self-control, she concentrated on keeping her expression composed.

"Lady Fallbrook and I have met before, but it has been more than a dozen years since I have had the pleasure of dancing with her. If you are not already engaged would you do me the honor of dancing the next with me?"

Shocked by the request, Emma hesitated for so long that the others began to regard her with curiosity.

Why was he doing this? she wondered frantically.

Perhaps she could understand the necessity of acknowledging each other, she thought, her mind casting about for a way to make sense of this unexpected situation. After all, they could not spend the rest of the Season ignoring one another. That behavior would soon set the gossips off and running.

But to dance with Jack Devruex? The idea seemed insupportable. The mere thought of touching him brought a hint of dizziness back.

His obsidian gaze held hers and a faint smile lurked at the corner of his mouth. Strangely, nothing in his expression bore any resemblance to the young man she had once loved. Dropping her gaze from his, she felt a hot blush rising to her cheeks. It was too soon to be able to react to his unexpected presence as if the past had not occurred.

But pretending just that appeared to be the only way to get through the next few minutes without making herself look ridiculous.

"I am not engaged, sir," she said, relieved and not a little surprised that her voice was so calm.

He held out his hand and the rapid beat of her heart forced her to take a few deep breaths before they moved to the floor. She slipped her gloved fingers into his large, warm hand and instantly recalled the first time she had done this. How young she had been, she thought wistfully, and how easily he had swept her away with his boyish good looks and devilish smile.

Well, the devilish smile was still there but there was no longer anything about him that could be called boyish, she thought as she sent him a quick glance.

The orchestra struck up a Viennese-style waltz, and Emma held her breath as his arm came around her waist. Her heart seemed to be firmly lodged in her throat and nothing, absolutely nothing, could force her to speak at this moment.

They danced in silence and the faces of the other guests went by in a blur. With near desperate determination she forced herself to concentrate on the music and ignore the feel of his broad shoulder beneath her hand.

His prowess as a dancer certainly had not changed, she observed, except possibly for improving. His effortless grace—and silence—as he guided her around the floor went a long way in helping her regain some of her composure.

Inhaling the elusive woodsy, smoky scent surrounding him, she told herself that this was not so terrible.

From now on Lord Devruex would just be someone with whom she would exchange the merest civilities should they find themselves near each other. Now that she had faced this initial encounter, she knew her own strength. Never again would Lord Devruex throw her, no matter how disturbing she found his presence.

"Do you find much changed since you were last in London, Lady Fallbrook?"

This was very good, she thought with relief at his polite words. They were just two civilized people, exchanging pleasantries. There would be no need to mention the painful past and for that she sent him a smile.

"Some of the new buildings are quite impressive, though it does seem as if the country is getting farther and farther away. I found the new theatre at Drury Lane a marvel of architecture."

"Yes, quite impressive. Speaking of the theatre, I hear that you caused quite a stir there yourself."

Taken by surprise, Emma could not help but laugh at the dry tease in his voice. "I did not, sir. Some wretched actor did. I thought my grandmother would call him out, she was so angered by his impertinence."

A slight smile curved the left corner of his lips. "But you

do not seem to find the incident as objectionable as the duchess did."

He guided her through a sweeping turn, and to her amazement, she found herself beginning to relax. That is, as long as she did not meet his unfathomable dark gaze. "No, I confess that I was taken aback at the time, but now I find the whole scene rather droll."

"Good for you."

The amused approval in his tone sent a warm flush through her body. It felt dreamlike to be in his arms again. This man, whom she once believed she knew so well, was now a complete stranger. Actually, when she thought about it, it would make this whole awkward situation easier if she did look at him as a stranger.

What had his life been like the last thirteen years? She wondered. By the looks of him, he had found success and satisfaction in life.

Something about his relaxed, confident mien reminded her of her black tomcat, Satin, sunning himself on the back terrace—utterly relaxed, utterly confident, and secure of his place in the world.

"Lady Emmaline, somehow you have managed to defy the passage of time and have grown even more beautiful since the last time I saw you."

Emma almost stumbled as his soft, deep voice rumbled over her body. At her near misstep his arm tightened around her ever so lightly to steady her. Instantly, the memory of that night on the muddy road rushed back and the pain and loss of the ensuing years stung her anew.

Anger rose within her, and lifting her chin, she met his dark gaze squarely. "Considering that the last time you saw me I was covered in mud and had not slept in almost two days, looking better is not such a great feat, even after thirteen years." If she had had a free hand she would have clapped it over her mouth to halt the sharp words from escaping her lips.

A flash of surprise crossed his face before he blinked his

black-as-sin eyes and his expression became closed and un-readable.

"You do have a point, my lady," he stated in an unper-turbed tone. "And your penchant for being disarmingly di-rect has certainly not diminished with the passing years either."

With excruciating embarrassment, Emma wondered what had happened to her. She had just congratulated her-self on her composure and civility, and an instant later, she lashed out at him in this horrid manner. Inwardly, she squirmed at knowing how she had given herself away. How pathetic he must think her, still bitter after thirteen years.

"I never did apologize to you, did I?"

His tone was light, almost amused, and the sudden desire to hit him choked the words in her throat.

Taking a ragged breath she wondered what insanity had suddenly run away with her senses. This was the last way she wanted to behave with him.

Without missing a single step, they continued to dance. She could not look at, nor answer, him and instead kept her gaze on the orchestra in the gallery.

"Admittedly thirteen years is a bit late, but please allow me to apologize for my part in our, shall I say, youthful foolishness. But all's well that ends well, as they say."

She pulled her gaze back to his as the room swirled around them. Nothing but lazy amusement glittered in his eyes, and in response, a searing anger had her gritting her teeth.

No, all did not end well; nothing had been truly well since that night, her thoughts shouted.

Despite the pain that his words caused, a deeply in-grained pride forced a smile to her lips.

Her marriage had taught her never to reveal her emo-tions, and thus, she excelled at feigning composure. If she had showed any emotional disturbance in front of Charles, he never ceased prodding her about it. He would harangue her, tirelessly trying to find a sore spot, until she felt she would scream. It had been much easier to learn to school her emotions than to be so passively tortured.

"Yes, we were so very young and foolish. And although it is not necessary after all these years, I accept your apology, Lord Devruex. And you are correct—all is well that ends well. We were very lucky to have come to our senses before embarking on what no doubt would have been a horrific mistake. There need not be any awkwardness between us should we meet again. After all, the past is the past and we are two civilized adults."

"I see we have the same opinion on the subject, Lady Fallbrook."

His cool, unperturbed tone caused a sharp pain near her heart and she sent up a prayer that the dance would end before she hit him or started to cry.

Her wish was granted moments later when, on one last sweeping turn, the music faded away and Lord Devruex bowed to her before leading her back to her grandmother. The expression on his strikingly masculine face remained polite and unreadable.

"Thank you, Lady Fallbrook."

Not trusting her voice, Emma inclined her head in reply as Lord Devruex took his leave of her.

Feeling angry, confused, and oddly deflated, she glanced down to see that her hands were trembling. Suddenly, this ball that she had anticipated with such eagerness could not end soon enough.

Chapter Six

Despite sleeping fitfully, Emma awakened early the next morning with thoughts of Jack Devruex and his amused dark eyes spinning in her head. Pushing herself up onto her elbows, she squinted and looked around her bed-chamber. Even though the heavy curtains were pulled across the long windows, leaving the room pleasantly dark, she gave up trying to sleep.

"This will not do," she groaned, kicking off the bed linens. Getting up, she stretched her arms high above her head, then bent down and touched her toes before ambling to the tall windows. Spreading the curtains wide, she gazed out to the lush back garden. The morning sun picked out glints of dew on the leaves and grass. Pushing her braid off her shoulder, she pressed her forehead against the cool pane and contemplated her peculiar mood.

Lord Devruex's unexpected appearance had shaken her usual confidence and self-possession, she admitted. How-ever, viewed in a charitable light, her discomfiture was really quite understandable. The drama of their final meeting and the heartbreak that followed had changed the path of her life. Despite the passage of so many years, it was only natural to have some kind of reaction to seeing him.

She just had not expected to have such a strong response, she thought, remembering her anger at his casual behavior during their dance.

The soft creak of the door drew her attention and she

turned to see Milton entering with a basket laden with flowers.

"How lovely," Emma said, grateful for the distraction.

"I knew you would be awake and stirring, my lady. And you'll be wanting to see all the lovely bouquets that have come for you already." Placing the basket on the table near the fireplace, the maid continued. "Shall I bring your breakfast, or will you be joining her grace?"

Picking up the first bunch of flowers, a mass of peonies, Emma said, "I shall have chocolate and toast here, and then I will go for a ride in Green Park. Please tell Wallace that I wish him to accompany me."

"Very good, my lady. A good gallop always puts the roses back in your cheeks. I will draw a bath for you. Will you wear your new habit?"

Shrugging her indifference, for she could not have given a fig for what she wore, Emma picked out the card nestling between the silky leaves. "Whatever you choose is fine," she said. As Milton left the room Emma moved to the chair by the fireplace. Gathering her ecru and blush lace wrap around her, she sat down and opened the envelope.

Until Thursday.
Darley

Emma smiled. He was such a charming and engaging man, and she reminded herself that she found him very attractive. She reached for the next bouquet—a mixture of fragrant spring flowers—and it took her a moment to find the card among the blooms.

To the Incomparable of Incomparables.
Monteford

Rolling her eyes, she said, "A bit over the top," and immediately set the card aside and reached for the next bouquet. It was a simple, though massive, bunch of gorgeous pink roses in bud, tied with a wide green grosgrain ribbon. The only thing on the ivory vellum card was *Devruex,* written in a firm, bold hand.

She stared at the card, her hand trembling ever so slightly. Picking up the roses, she breathed deeply of their alluring scent and wondered why he had sent them. The feel of dancing with him came back in a heady wave. The breadth of his shoulders and the feel of his strong arms filled her senses again. Her breathing quickened as a rush of piercing anger hit her full force.

The feeling held her in its grip for several moments before she made herself set the flowers and card aside. In an attempt to gain control of her wayward emotions, she said aloud, "This is ridiculous. I will stop thinking of him."

Since early childhood she had been able to school her emotions to her needs and this time would be no different, she told herself sternly.

After breakfast, she bathed and dressed in the new riding habit. Tugging on a fine pair of gloves, she turned to Milton and said, "Please put the peonies and the roses in vases."

"What about the other flowers?" Milton asked.

"I had forgotten about those. Do whatever you'd like with them. I care not," Emma instructed over her shoulder as she left the room.

On the other side of town, Sally Willoughby crumpled the note she had just received from one of Lady Colhurst's footmen. She had paid handsomely for the information, and to her great infuriation, she trusted every word.

"Rivers! *RIVERS!*" she screamed at the top of her lungs as she ran up the stairs, cursing under her breath between shouts.

"Yes, ma'am?"

Reaching the landing, she whipped around to see her stone-faced butler gazing up at her from the foyer.

"Where have you been? Didn't you hear me calling you?" She hated it when her servants were less than perfect.

The butler's shoulders rose slightly as he let out a long-suffering sigh. "Yes, I heard you. I apologize, ma'am. What may I do for you?"

"I want the gig brought around now. I am going to the park."

"Very good, Mrs. Wil—"

She turned away before he finished and stomped down the hall to her bedchamber. Upon entering the room, she saw her maid laying out her green walking gown and matching pelisse.

"I hate him!" Sally shouted and slammed the door.

"Now, ma'am, do not be gettin' yourself in a state. You know you'll just start crying and make your face red and puffy."

"I am too angry to cry! I hate him, I hate him, I hate him! He cancels an evening with me to go to that ball and dance with Lady Fallbrook. After what happened at the theatre, it is an insult! And who is she anyway? She dresses oddly and is at least five years older than me!" She kicked her shoes off with such force that they sailed across the room, sending a crystal candy dish crashing to the floor.

Cooper lifted her shoulders in a resigned shrug. "Well, she's quality and very rich. Everyone knows his lordship is hurting for blunt and needs to be looking for a wife who is plump in the pockets," she stated as she began to help her mistress off with her morning gown.

"Ha! Shows what you know," Sally snapped. "The Montefords are rich enough. He just doesn't know how to manage his mama. Oh, why couldn't I have captured Devruex? He makes me shiver and his money is his own."

The stout servant made no comment and Sally continued in a less strident tone of voice. "You are going to have to find out about that Fallbrook woman."

Cooper sniffed and retrieved the green gown from the bed. "I don't know anyone at the Duchess of Kelbourne's household. 'Tis going to cost you more than a dress or two to get anyone to tell me anything," she said as she pulled the gown over Sally's head.

"I don't care!" came the muffled cry from beneath the gown as she shoved her arms through the sleeves. "I have to know if Monteford sees her again. How dare she try to poach my man," she said as her head emerged through the neck.

Cooper snorted and shook her head. "That ain't how things work an' you know it. If she wants 'im, you don't matter. What does a lady care about the likes of you? Ouch!"

"Keep saying things like that and I'll pinch you again!" Sally shouted.

Rubbing her arm, Cooper shrugged. "I ain't saying nothing that ain't true. You are going to get yourself in trouble if you go treating the nibs disrespectful. Then where will you be?"

"Hush and help me get ready. If I don't get out of this house I shall go mad," she ordered, turning to her vanity table.

Less than an hour later, Mrs. Willoughby was tooling her shiny red gig, with its perfectly matched white ponies, through Green Park. She had no desire to go to Hyde Park, which was always more crowded and where she was likely to be recognized. Her ponies were so well-trained, and knew the route so well, that she barely needed to pay them any attention as she mulled over her disturbing thoughts.

She was still stewing about that Fallbrook woman and Monteford.

After all, she was the famous Sally Willoughby, toasted as an Incomparable from one end of Town to the other. Didn't he have any idea how many men desired her? Didn't he know how crowds gathered at her front door just to catch a glimpse of her? Monteford should be kissing her feet for deigning to bestow her favors upon him, she thought bitterly.

As the little conveyance trundled along the smooth lane that delimited the park, a new and disturbing thought presented itself. What if he threw her over for Lady Fallbrook?

It would be one thing if he married the average, dull, mealymouthed Society woman—Sally would not feel threatened by such a creature.

But it would be quite another thing if he chose someone like Lady Fallbrook. When their eyes had met briefly at the theatre, Sally had instantly recognized the pride and strength in the lady's features. She did not look like she would tolerate her husband squiring his flashy mistress around Town.

Monteford would not get rid of her, she assured herself stubbornly, gripping the leather reins tightly. Yes, they had a contract, but he was a lord, and she was not so naïve to believe that any court would uphold such an agreement.

Two years ago, when she embarked upon this path, her intentions had been to salt away as much money as possible and gain her independence. But her life had not turned out as she had intended. She passionately loved having all her bills paid and spending her sizable allowance, but there were *so* many pretty bits and pieces that caught her fancy and she loved to entertain lavishly.

In truth, she had almost no money in reserve and she suddenly felt vulnerable about her future. Of course, she had the jewels, but they never fetched as much as they were worth. As she continued driving along in the warm spring air, she realized that from here on out she was going to have to be very careful.

A horse and rider running flat out across the open stretch of grass before her caught her attention. Rarely had Sally witnessed a woman using a sidesaddle ride with such reckless skill. Impressed, Sally kept her gaze on the woman and horse, envying her ability. As they drew closer, Sally suddenly recognized the profile.

"Think of the devil, or whatever," she said aloud and flicked the ribbons to urge her ponies forward.

Of course Lady Fallbrook would be an excellent horse-woman, she thought bitterly. Lady Fallbrook probably excelled at every ladylike skill one could think of. The *perfectly perfect* Lady Fallbrook, she thought resentfully as she steered the gig to intersect with her rival.

Without thinking past the next moment, she lifted her green-gloved hand and waved at Lady Fallbrook, who was still riding at a bruising run. It took a few moments of vigorous gesticulations before she was sure she had attracted her attention. Lady Fallbrook slowed the horse, turned his direction slightly, and began to trot toward her.

Sally eyed the lady's dove gray and lavender riding habit, smarting with jealousy at the elegance of the original design. The short lavender jacket was a feminine version of a gentleman's frock coat and her gray silk tricorne hat had a short, sheer veil as its only adornment. The ensemble, right down to the elegant knot in the stock at her throat, looked simple yet dashing.

Sally clenched her teeth against her rising ire, for she herself had been hailed as the standard of what was fashionable and abhorred the idea of anyone usurping that role.

Lady Fallbrook brought her horse to a stop a little distance away. Her expression showed no emotion except polite self-assurance. Sally felt her anger rise higher, for no matter how she tried she had never been able to emulate the poise and composure that the upper classes wore so naturally.

Doing her best to perform a bow from her seat in the gig, Sally said, "Good morning, Lady Fallbrook. I wonder if you might honor me with a moment of your time."

Looking down at her, Lady Fallbrook remained silent for a moment before saying, "I do not believe I have had the pleasure of making your acquaintance."

How did she do it? Sally asked herself with a feeling of seething vexation. Her tone was so courteous one could be-

lieve that Lady Fallbrook was used to being confronted by
notorious courtesans.

But that very politeness caused a frisson of alarm to rush
up Sally's spine. It would be foolish to forget that this
woman wielded power in the world. After all, Lady Fallbrook was the sister of the Duke of Kelbourne. The words
of her maid cautioning her not to disrespect the nibs came
rushing back.

But now that her rival was before her, meeting her gaze
with an expression of polite—and very faint—curiosity,
Sally's inherent sense of pride and sudden insecurity about
her future urged her to reckless measures.

"Why, I am Mrs. Willoughby. And you are Lady Fallbrook. Could we, perhaps, move to that little stand of trees
and get out of the sun? I am sure neither one of us would
like to risk getting freckles."

After an instant of hesitation, Lady Fallbrook said, "If
you would like, Mrs. Willoughby."

There it was again, that damned unflappable civility,
Sally thought. She got down from the gig as Lady Fallbrook
gracefully slid down from her horse. Sally left the gig
where it was, knowing the ponies would happily graze on
the grass and not wander far. She followed as Lady Fallbrook led her horse to the trees and, finding a low branch,
secured the animal before turning to Sally.

"I confess you have me rather curious, Mrs.
Willoughby."

They stood on the grass facing each other beneath the
spreading branches, the balmy morning air ruffling the
transparent veil covering the top half of Lady Fallbrook's
face.

Sally lifted her chin and took the plunge. "I shall not
waste your time, my lady. You are aware that Lord Monteford and I have an understanding. I would ask that you respect our relationship."

Sally realized her nerves had made her tone more abrupt
than she intended. *What have I done?* Sally wondered in

rising panic. She cursed her willful temper, for she knew full well that if it became known that she had so much as said good morning to someone of Lady Fallbrook's ilk, Monteford would send her packing in a flash.

Furthermore, this insulting action could also jeopardize her chances with other gentlemen in the future—after all, a member of the demimonde should know her place.

It was too late to take back the words now, she thought with trepidation. Holding her breath, she waited for Lady Fallbrook's reaction.

A moment later, she bit back a growl of frustration. Lady Fallbrook's expression did not change a whit. *How do you do it?* she wanted to scream.

"You really do think of yourself as Queen Willow, don't you?" Lady Fallbrook said softly.

The detached amusement in her voice infuriated Sally, and any lingering fear evaporated in the face of it. "What can you know of my life? You, who have never struggled, never wanted for anything. The *perfectly perfect* Lady Fallbrook," she finished with a sneer.

The subtle change that came over Lady Fallbrook's features caused Sally's fear to return in spades. One delicately arched brow rising over a dark blue eye had Sally cursing her wayward temper again. Lady Fallbrook could express more with that one little movement than Sally could with her whole body.

"Since this is a most unusual situation, I shall set aside my natural tendency to give the cut direct to rude people and only say that you know nothing of my life either. But because I am feeling oddly generous this morning, I will tell you that I am not the least bit interested in Lord Monteford. I find Lord Darley much more attractive."

Sally stared at the elegant woman, for once speechless. Everything in Lady Fallbrook's poised manner showed that she did not give a sixpence for Sally's fears, yet Sally found it almost impossible to believe that she did not want Monteford.

She opened her mouth to reply, when a movement behind Lady Fallbrook caught her eye. Tilting her head to the side, she saw a horse emerge from the stand of trees. Catching her breath, she saw Lord Devruex astride the great black beast. From beneath his angled beaver topper, he looked at her with glittering dark eyes and she found his expression as haughty and unreadable as Lady Fallbrook's.

Suddenly, Sally felt completely out of her depth. It was one thing to take on her rival woman to woman, but having a witness—and one as powerful as Devruex—was quite another thing.

"Lord Devruex! How lovely to see you on this fine morning," she said in a rush as she moved swiftly to her gig. "I am sure you know Lady Fallbrook. I must fly now. Good day."

She sent one last glance to Lady Fallbrook and almost stopped in her tracks at the look of stunned vulnerability that came across her face.

Feeling satisfaction at Lady Fallbrook's sudden discomfiture, Sally spared a moment to wonder what had cracked that cold façade before she quit the scene.

Chapter Seven

After watching Mrs. Willoughby rush to her gig in a flurry of green muslin, Emma turned to look at Jack Devruex in surprise and dread. Evidently, everyone she did not wish to see had risen early this morning, she thought with vexation, wondering if he had overheard any of her extremely strange conversation with Mrs. Willoughby.

He sat astride the most beautiful horse she had ever seen. The beast danced and tossed its beautifully shaped head, as if to show himself to better advantage. Her gaze shifted to Devruex and she noted that his riding clothes were exquisitely tailored—which had not been the case thirteen years ago.

The jacket, made of a charcoal superfine, accented his flawless pale skin and dark eyes. As a soft breeze fluttered her short veil, her gaze was drawn to the way his buckskin breeches defined his muscular thighs.

"Making new friends?" he asked as he agilely dismounted and tossed the reins over the pommel.

At his droll query, Emma surprised herself by laughing. "I doubt Mrs. Willoughby would say so. What are you doing here, Lord Devruex?" She knew her tone was peremptory, but after her disturbing confrontation with Mrs. Willoughby, she did not feel equipped to deal with the even more disturbing baron.

He gave a negligent shrug. "I often take a morning gallop. But I shall confess that when I saw London's most famous lady and most infamous courtesan in conversation, I had to make a closer inspection in case my eyes had hoaxed me."

At his sophisticated banter, she felt tongue-tied and awkward. The reality of seeing him twice in less than twenty-four hours overwhelmed her senses. She felt a hot blush flushing her cheeks, but strangely, it was not from embarrassment, but anger—the same inexplicable anger she had felt last night when they danced together and again this morning when she had received his flowers.

Picking up the train of her habit, she moved toward her horse. In the distance, she saw her groom, Wallace, walking his mount by the pond. He probably assumed she had arranged this assignation and was keeping a respectful distance, she thought with some exasperation.

"Too bad it wasn't Darley who had the good fortune to come upon you," Jack continued in a tone full of mild amusement as he moved to lean against a tree, his dark gaze never leaving her face. "I assure you, at this moment, he would be exceedingly gratified."

So he had heard her comment about finding Lord Darley attractive. She did not care, she thought with a lift of her chin. It instantly sprang to her mind that there had been a time when Jack Devruex would not have been so sanguine about her finding another man attractive.

"Do you think so?" she asked coldly.

He eyed her with thinly veiled amusement mixed with curiosity. "Lady Fallbrook, I must say I find your behavior toward me rather troublesome. You have claimed that the past has been laid to rest, yet I would swear that you are angry with me about something. I cannot imagine what it could be since we have not so much as exchanged a greeting in thirteen years."

Taken aback by his perceptive remarks, Emma honestly did not know how to reply. Inexplicably, her anger grew. "I am not angry, sir. What an odd notion."

He made an offhand gesture and she noticed the strong length of his fingers. "Nevertheless, there it is."

With an impatient movement, she kicked her train behind her and wondered why she just did not leave. "Because I do not fawn over you like some silly girl just out of the schoolroom does not mean I am angry."

She had been such a creature once, she thought with bitter self-recrimination—never again.

He kept his glittering dark gaze on hers for a long moment. Soon she found his speculative attention too unsettling and had to look away from his disturbingly masculine face. She was beginning to resent his effortless ability to disconcert her.

"What has brought you to London after all these years?" he asked in a different tone of voice.

Again, she did not quite know how to reply. "I have grown rather bored with country life," she said after a long pause.

He pushed away from the tree. His black boots, gleaming in the clear morning light, echoed the gleam in his dark eyes. "Are you aware that you have instantly become all the rage? They are already laying odds at White's on whom you will marry."

"Men will throw their money away on the most ridiculous things," she said with an amused shake of her head. "Who is the favorite?"

"Right now? Monteford. But if I lay some blunt on Darley the odds are sure to change."

"Then you will all lose for I have no intention of marrying anyone," she stated firmly.

A dark brow arched up in surprise, making his expression even more devilish. "Then you find Darley attractive for things other than matrimony?"

Sending him a haughty look through her sheer veil, she said, "Not that it is any of your business."

"You are right, of course, but it's not the first time I have overreached myself. However, if it's a bit of romance you're after, why not leave the field open to the rest of us?"

Emma gaped at him, hardly believing she had heard his casually spoken words correctly.

"You? Never!"

"Now, see, when you shout like that it makes me believe that you are angry, despite your avowals to the contrary. Why not me? Unless your tastes have changed so much that you now care only for blonds? Or *are* you still angry with me?"

She really could have hit him. She fumed as she struggled to keep her expression from revealing her true emotions. The last thing she wanted was for him to realize how much his lazy teasing affected her confused senses. Again, the vision of her black cat came to mind, only this time Satin was toying with a mouse.

Clenching her kid-gloved hands together, she sent him what she hoped was a look of haughty indifference. "Gracious. I've not been in Town a full week—I'm not sure what kind of adventure I want yet. But I assure you, I shall make every effort to enjoy myself while I find out."

His urbane, amused expression froze for an instant and she watched his square jaw tighten. Lost in the intensity of unidentifiable emotions, she wasn't aware for a moment that he had moved closer.

At the look in his eyes, a flutter of feminine instinct sent her backing away from him. Turning, she took quick strides to her horse, grateful that she had tied him near a stump so that she could mount unaided.

Nerves spurred her to quickness and once she was atop the chestnut mare, she swung the horse around to see that Jack had not moved.

He stood beneath the tree, gazing up at her. He bowed, and she thought there was something gently mocking in the movement. A hint of a smile had the dimples creasing his cheeks.

Pressing her heel against her horse's flank, she said,

"Thank you for the beautiful flowers, Lord Devruex. Good day."

As she galloped away, his rich, deep laughter followed her.

Chapter Eight

Frederick Litton, Viscount Monteford, trudged up the curving staircase that led to his grandfather's private study. With a heavy sense of foreboding, he reached the landing and paused to look at himself in the ornately framed mirror hanging on the hallway wall.

He wanted to make sure that not even a speck of lint marred his snuff brown coat and that his simply tied neckcloth was not unduly limp. He frowned at his reflection, not really liking the garment's conservative lapel and cuffs, but grandfather disliked any article of clothing that appeared excessively fashionable.

Glancing down, he saw with relief that his boots had not attracted any dust on his short walk from the drive. Straightening his shoulders, he continued down the wide hall, passing portrait after portrait of his ancestors, but did not hurry his steps.

He'd get there soon enough, he thought resentfully. As much as he dreaded this meeting—dreaded it as soon as he had received the brief, coldly worded missive that morning—he was determined to stand up to the old man this time.

As he drew near, the footmen standing on either side of the imposing double doors bowed in unison before opening them. Without changing the tempo of his stride, he walked into the octagonal-shaped room and took a deep breath. In the middle of the grand space, behind a massive mahogany desk, sat the Earl of Pellerton.

Monteford noted that the earl's thick shock of white hair showed little sign of thinning. Another infuriating sign of his grandfather's apparent agelessness, he thought resentfully.

He could judge the condition of his grandfather's pate because the old man had not lifted his head from the papers he perused. Standing at near attention in front of the desk, Monteford took care not to shift his weight or slouch.

As he waited to be noticed, he wondered what he would have to promise this time before he was allowed to again live his life in peace.

Raising his gaze to the ceiling, he studied the realistically painted hunting scene and cursed the unfairness of his circumstances. He'd much rather be calling upon the enigmatic and beautiful Lady Fallbrook. Last night, when they had danced the quadrille, he had been a little surprised at her cool demeanor. After all, when their eyes had met across the theatre he had experienced an immediate attraction. Ladies treating him coolly was not something he had a lot of experience with, and his interest in her was more than piqued.

The complimentary note he had sent along with his floral tribute this morning should certainly have impressed her, he thought with satisfaction.

The rustling of parchment continued for several more minutes before the earl finally set the sheaf on the neatly organized desktop.

The old man raised his head and fixed Monteford with his gaze, his expression bereft of any discernable emotion.

"Thank you for being prompt, Monteford. You may pull that chair a little closer to the desk," he said in a strong voice with a hint of a rasp.

"Yes, sir," Monteford replied in his most respectful tone and did as the earl directed.

Once seated, he did his best to wait patiently for his

grandfather to explain the reason for his peremptory summons. To do otherwise would only prolong the visit.

The earl leaned back in his chair, crossed his hands over his chest and pronounced, "In the last week I have been the recipient of no less than four visits from your mother."

Ah, the situation was becoming clearer. "Am I to understand, by the tone of your voice, that you did not desire these visits, Grandfather?"

The earl eyed him charily and Monteford cautioned himself to tread carefully and keep any hint of sarcasm from his voice. His grandfather would pounce like a falcon if he suspected any hint of disrespect from his grandson and heir.

Despite the earl's advanced years, no one in the large Litton family doubted that his faculties were as still as sharp as ever and that he wielded ultimate authority over almost every aspect of their lives, especially the financial aspect.

"Under ordinary circumstances I welcome the occasional visit from my daughter-in-law. However, it is most distressing to receive her when she is near hysterical," he said with a tone of accusation lacing his voice.

"Hysterical, sir? This is indeed disturbing news. May I inquire as to what has caused my mother such anxiety?"

At this innocent question the earl's upper lip curled in a contemptuous sneer. "Playing coy is unbecoming to a gentleman, boy. But if you insist, I will put the unseemly truth into words. Your mother is taken by the hysterics because of the manner in which you are making a byword of yourself by flaunting your doxy among Polite Society. No less distressing is the money you throw away on her keep. By gad, she lives better than a queen."

At this blunt speech, Monteford swallowed hard, and struggled to keep his nervous hands motionless. "Sir, I would hate to revisit this very old argument. If I had my own income, this issue would not—"

"Own income!" the earl rasped in mounting fury. "Any amount of money I would settle upon you would be gone before the Season ended. You have been bleeding me for years, but it is going to cease. You are almost five and thirty—"

"Six and thirty," Monteford interjected without thinking.

The earl's look of contempt made Monteford feel like squirming. "Even worse, boy! I am not going to keep throwing my money down a poisoned well. Enough is enough. It would not be so bad if you at least did something to improve the situation. Why can you not be more like your friend Devruex? He overcame his straitened circumstances by being clever and wanting to do his family name proud instead of dragging it through the mud."

A familiar stab of anger and jealousy pierced Monteford at his grandfather's praise of Devruex. He had to listen to comments like this during most of his encounters with his grandfather. As much as Monteford admired Devruex, at moments like this he could almost hate him.

"Believe me, sir, Devruex is very far from being an angel," he said, attempting a dismissive chuckle.

"Angel? Who cares about angels? Devruex had a bad hand dealt by his dissolute father. Shameful business. But Devruex never let the side down."

Monteford felt his temper begin to seethe, but said nothing. By long experience he knew it was much better not to gainsay the old man.

"Do not delude yourself, boy," the earl continued. "From this moment your life has changed. You are going to marry as soon as may be. Besides the need to settle down, it is past time for you to provide an heir. I will not allow the earldom to be entailed out of the direct line."

Monteford stared at his grandfather in alarm. It was one thing to sit through the ignominy of a dressing down, but never before had his grandfather made such a direct threat.

"I mean no disrespect, sir, but I have no desire to marry and as we do not live in medieval times I can see no way for you to force me."

"Don't you? Then you are not nearly as astute as I thought. Do not mistake me—if you do not do your duty, I shall cut you off immediately. In fact, as of today, you are cut off without a farthing until you present me with your future wife. I suspect that you will not like the idea of your tailor bandying about Town that you cannot pay for your newest waistcoat."

Monteford felt his clenched fingers grow cold as his grandfather eyed him with icy resolve. He knew he had been pushing his luck when he had agreed to take Sally to Drury Lane, but he never suspected that his grandfather would react so vehemently.

Feeling desperate, Monteford could think of nothing to say to soften his grandfather's attitude.

"I suggest that you start looking around for a bride," the earl said in a calmer tone. "It should not be too difficult. There is any number of suitable ladies in Town this Season."

By *suitable*, Monteford knew the old man meant *wealthy*. Suddenly, just when he felt he would drown in his grandfather's despotic control, the vision of sea blue eyes and beautiful serene features came to mind. The moment their eyes had met across the theatre he had known there was something unique about Lady Fallbrook, not the least of which was the rumored size of her fortune.

"Lady Fallbrook," he said in an unthinking whisper.

The earl slapped the desk with a resounding thwack. "That's the spirit! Good gracious me! If you could marry one such as Lady Fallbrook, I would settle ten thousand pounds upon you! Tell me, have you managed an introduction? If not, I am well acquainted with the dowager Duchess of Kelbourne."

"We have met. In fact, sir," Monteford said, beginning to warm to the idea, "we danced at Lady Colhurst's ball last night. I have every reason to believe that she will not discourage my interest."

As he recalled her surprisingly direct gaze, his heart began to pound at the thought of being completely free from his grandfather's control. The look sparkling in his grandfather's heretofore frosty eyes suddenly made him feel more than halfway in love with the fashionable widow.

"This is excellent, Monteford. Most excellent. Lady Fallbrook is a perfect choice."

"Thank you, Grandfather. Now that we have an understanding, there is the matter of my boot maker. . . ."

The earl wagged a long, bony finger at his grandson. "No, I shall stand firm, boy, or you will backslide. As soon as you present me with your future wife, all will be well. Now off with you."

Chapter Nine

"Grandmère, would you mind if I cried off shopping with you this afternoon? I have a stack of correspondence that I would like to read," Emma asked, as she and her grandmother lingered over their luncheon.

Grandmère preferred this room, the west-facing salon decorated in shades of cream and gold, when they dined privately, for it was smaller and slightly less formal than the dining room.

"I would not mind at all, my dear," Grandmère said over her teacup. "I just hope you have not received a letter from that man managing your school saying that it is falling apart without you."

Emma laughed and said, "I am sure it is not. I found very proficient people to take care of the everyday running of the school."

"No doubt you did. You have always displayed impressive organizational skills. No, you have probably received a packet of billet-doux from all the gentlemen you slayed last night. Or did you receive them this morning with all those flowers I saw your maid carrying upstairs," she said with a knowing twinkle in her lovely eyes.

"Lord Monteford's note called me the 'Incomparable of Incomparables.'" Emma tried to keep a straight face as she relayed this information but failed at her grandmother's derisive snort.

"Just like Monteford to do the thing much too brown. I'd

wager that Devruex did not go so over the top if he sent you a tribute."

Emma's fingers stilled on the delicate handle of her cup. "Lord Devruex sent a bouquet of pink roses. By your comment, I could almost believe that you like him."

"I do," Grandmère quickly rejoined, setting her fork precisely on the edge of her plate. "I may be old, but I am not blind. Devruex is as fine an example of masculinity as you'll ever find. He is just like his grandfather, who was one of the singularly most rapscallion men of my generation—but madly charming for all that. Devruex's grandfather could ride the hounds all day, dance all night, challenge someone to a duel at dawn, and start it all again the next day. His grandson is cut from the same cloth. And Devruex has exquisite manners. He calls upon me at least once every Season."

"Does he really?" Emma never would have believed it, especially since Grandmère had never mentioned Devruex in any of her letters.

Nevertheless, though she never revealed her youthful indiscretion with Jack Devruex, Emma had always had a small suspicion that Mama had told Grandmère of the near disastrous event.

"Yes," Grandmère continued. "He always stays above half an hour and has the very flattering gift of flirting back."

"Grandmère!"

"Don't come off all prudish with me, my girl. Not after your talk of paramours," the old lady said with a wag of her finger. "Seriously, I have always enjoyed Devruex. He has become quite the nonpareil in the horse-breeding world. Harwich says Devruex has an unerring eye when it comes to prime horseflesh. One of Devruex's horses is entered in the Severly Stakes next month and Harwich is going to place a wager for me."

Setting her cup back in its saucer, Emma said softly, "Building a racing stable was always one of his dreams."

Realizing that she had just revealed far too much, Emma cast a quick, nervous look to her grandmother and sent up a prayer that the keen old lady hadn't noticed.

"Is that so, my dear? How very interesting. Now off you go to read your letters" was all she said, to Emma's great relief.

Quickly, she did as her grandmother instructed. Setting aside her napkin, she rose from her chair and after pressing a quick kiss on her grandmother's cheek, she left the room.

Once in the sitting room next to her bedchamber, Emma moved to the pale blue velvet covered settee next to the large window. With a feeling of relief—for she needed something to distract her chaotic thoughts from Jack Devruex—she picked up the first letter in the stack on the small table next to the settee and saw by the familiar handwriting that it was from her mother.

Breaking the black wax seal, she noted that the return address was Brighton. Settling comfortably on the settee, she unfolded the sheets.

> *My dearest love,*
> *By the time you receive this I trust that you will be settled with your grandmother in Town and have begun a new chapter in your life. I am so pleased that you have finally emerged from your genteel exile in Yorkshire and are now taking pleasure in the delights of London.*
> *You must make every effort to enjoy yourself, but I do know how imperious my mother-in-law can be and urge you not to allow her to bully you unduly. Not that I would ever begrudge her your company.*
> *I hope you will not be too surprised to learn that I shall not be traveling to London this year. I fear my poor nerves would be ripped to shreds in all that noise and soot. No, dear Emmaline, I am quite content to stay by the sea with my friends.*
> *You will be happy to know that a letter from your*

*brother arrived yesterday and he informs me that he
and Julia are enjoying Italy prodigiously. How I miss
them!*

*And only today I received a letter from our dear
friend Lady Grafton, who is also in Town. She informs me that you are setting the fashion with your
dashing bonnets and the cut of your pelisses. How diverting, my love. May I ask when you suddenly developed such a keen taste for fashion?*

*Pray write to me and tell me how you find London
and if you have met any exceptional gentleman. The
only thing that your grandmother and I agree upon is
that you should marry again.*

*I shall close for now and look forward to your next
letter.*

Your loving Mama

With an amused smile at the marriage reference, Emma
set her mother's letter aside and reached for the next note.
A quick perusal revealed that it was from Amelia and written that very morning. Taking a moment to admire the
pretty handwriting, she read:

Emma,
*I write to beg you to come to dinner unfashionably
early this evening. It has been so long since we have
had a good gossip and I shall endeavor to persuade
Penelope to arrive early as well. Will the promise of
an adventure later in the evening bring you to us before the usual hour? If so, I suggest you take a nap
this afternoon, for my husband and I intend to keep
you up quite late.*

Emma glanced over at the mantel clock and decided that
a nap would be just the thing, for she felt unusually fatigued

after being out so late last night and experiencing the disturbing events of the morning.

Not bothering to ring for her maid, she kicked off her slippers and managed to undo enough buttons on her afternoon gown to remove it by herself. Tossing the garment over the back of a chair, she crossed the room to the windows and pulled the drapery partially closed to dim the room.

Once settled beneath a light green satin coverlet on the downy bed, she closed her eyes and concentrated on her plans for the church bazaar in the autumn. Back home, the festive weekend, always one of the highlights of the year, took months of detailed preparations to ensure its success.

To her great vexation, glittering black eyes and broad shoulders intruded upon every thought. No matter how she tossed and turned she could not vanquish Jack Devruex from her mind.

Everything about him confused and angered her—especially angered her. This was quite odd, for nothing ever angered her.

What did he mean by saying that if she was looking for romance she should leave the field open? She mulled over his outrageous comment as she punched the feather pillow.

He was a stranger to her, no matter what had transpired between them years ago. She knew nothing of the life he had lived after he had broken her heart. Broken her heart and left her to a life she had, at eighteen, never imagined she could endure.

Yet she could not deny that there was something completely, agonizingly familiar about Jack Devruex. Frowning, she tried to sort her jumbled thoughts. He was not necessarily familiar in the physical sense, for he was quite different from the near boy she had known. No, what was familiar was how she felt when she looked into his eyes.

Beneath the inexplicable anger that assailed her senses when he was near stirred the feelings he had awakened in her the first time they met. Feelings that she had told herself were a figment of her imagination during the last thirteen years. Charles had certainly never made her feel this thrilling awareness of exciting and unknown possibilities.

Kicking off the coverlet, she sat up and looked across the room to the massive bouquet of pink roses Milton had placed upon the petite desk.

It suddenly occurred to her that she had not been completely honest last night when she had proclaimed to her grandmother that Charles had never hurt her. In truth, he had. Not deeply, not permanently, but enough to have taught her a powerful truth.

For she had realized early in her marriage that Charles's petty attacks would have been devastating if she had loved him. If she had ever loved her husband the way she had once loved Jack Devruex, the desolation of their marriage would have left her an empty hull of her former self.

A shiver traveled over her flesh as she stared at the flowers.

She must cease these painful and futile regrets. Life had taught her too well how pointless it was to look back. It was beyond foolish to permit any lingering, wistful memories of what might have been to throw her into confusion.

Feeling her unsettled emotions beginning to calm, she relaxed again into the sumptuous bedding, and finally fell into a restless slumber.

Chapter Ten

Because she was quite curious about Amelia's mysteriously worded invitation, Emma had not minded having to dress earlier than expected, for it was a welcome distraction from her muddled thoughts. She was growing quite frustrated, for it seemed that no matter how much she reasoned with herself, she could not forget the feeling of looking into Jack Devruex's eyes.

At least Grandmère had not noticed anything amiss when they had met in the foyer before she left for her musical evening at Lady Burlton's.

Using the time in the coach to take herself in hand, Emma felt much more her usual sanguine self when she reached the Spence-Jones' fashionable townhouse in Cavendish Square.

Upon entering Amelia's salon, which was exquisitely decorated in the latest Chinese style, she saw that Penelope had also managed to get herself ready early for the evening—quite a feat for the countess, who was notorious for her tardiness.

"Now isn't this lovely?" Amelia said after greetings were exchanged. "I shall tell you of our plans for the evening and then we shall have a nice gossip before the other guests arrive."

With glasses of sherry in hand, the ladies walked to the French doors leading to the Spence-Jones's beautifully landscaped, terraced garden. The sun had not completely finished with the day and still cast a purple-and-orange glow over the lush space.

"You have arranged for a perfect evening, Amelia," Penelope said as they all stood looking out over the garden, the heady scent of gardenias wafting around them.

"Yes, perfect. We shall be a merry party," Amelia began, looking flushed with excitement. "I am so glad I persuaded you to arrive early, Emma, for I wanted to let you in on our plan before the others arrive. Penelope has already heard."

Emma lifted her glass to her hostess. "No need to persuade me to do anything. You desired my presence now, so here I am. I confess you have me on tenterhooks of anticipation about your plans." Because of Amelia's obvious excitement about the evening, Emma decided to wait until later to tell them about her bizarre encounter with Mrs. Willoughby. She had already decided not to share her unexpected meeting with Devruex; she felt too confused about her inexplicable reaction to speak of him.

Amelia led them down onto the next terrace and they seated themselves in comfortable wicker chairs. Emma thought her friends looked beautiful. Penelope complemented the sunset in her glowing gown of bronze-and-apricot silk and Amelia's milky complexion and dark hair showed to advantage in her layers of strawberry satin.

Emma again had left her choice of evening wear to Milton, who had presented her mistress with a sophisticated confection of icy blue silk, net, and seed pearls. The gown was lovely, but the little cap sleeves looked so delicate Emma wondered if they would stay up. However, here in the balmy dusk she was pleased with the garment.

Taking a deep breath of the perfumed air, Emma looked at her friends expectantly, and noted a look of concern in Penelope's large green eyes.

"There will be only eight of us tonight," Amelia began. "When everyone arrives we shall all go on the merriest silliest frolic. My dearest husband has arranged for us to spend the evening at Vauxhall Gardens!"

"Vauxhall Gardens!" Emma had once harbored a desire to visit the famed pleasure gardens but Charles refused her request to attend when they had come to London during their marriage.

Before that, during her first Season, Jack had promised to take her. *Why do I remember things like that?* she chided herself as Amelia continued.

"I know you must be wondering what has become of our senses. Our set has always thought the place too crowded, too overblown. I admit the whole atmosphere is rather over the top. But that's just what we are all in the mood for, don't you think?"

Emma laughed with pleasure at Amelia's charming enthusiasm. "Yes, I think that sounds perfect on this warm eve. A bit of over-the-top fun will keep us all from becoming too stiff-necked and pleased with ourselves."

"Oh, I was hoping you would say that! If you go along in the proper spirit of the thing, then so will everyone else. I've been in such a mood for a good romp. We will have a grand time, don't you think?"

"I do. I too am desirous of a good romp, as you so succinctly put it," Emma agreed.

"I would not be so sure about that," Penelope, sitting across from Emma, put in. "Amelia, tell Emma who shall make up our party."

Emma sent Penelope a questioning look, as Amelia set her glass down on a nearby table and began counting off the guests on her fingers. "Well, there is Roger and I. Penelope and Tunbridge. Emma, of course. Mr. Robert Bosworth and his sister, Mrs. Dorothea Bruce. They are the grandchildren of the Earl of Nottingham. I believe you are acquainted with that family. And the charming Baron Devruex rounds out our merry troupe."

Emmaline, in the act of reaching for her glass of sherry, knocked it over at the mention of Jack's name.

Jack Devruex! That explained Penelope's mysterious comment.

"How clumsy of me. I'm so sorry." With a quick movement, she righted the glass, grateful the liquid had not splashed on her gown.

Frantically casting about for something to say, she glanced from the beautiful garden, basking in the last glow of the setting sun, into the drawing room, where the servants were busily lighting the chandelier and performing the final preparations before the other guests arrived.

He would arrive anytime now, she thought in rising panic.

The thought of a whole evening spent in his presence, after what occurred in Green Park that morning, was intolerable. But how to extricate herself from this awful situation without upsetting Amelia? Biting her lip, she looked at her friend's smiling face. Under any other circumstances she would never consider bowing out of a social obligation, especially to such a good friend.

Well, needs must, she told herself. "Amelia, I hate to upset you, but I must beg off tonight."

"What? You must be teasing me," Amelia looked flabbergasted.

With an inward sigh, Emma realized she would not so easily make her escape.

"I would not tease on such a subject. In truth, I-I do not care for Lord Devruex and would much rather avoid making anyone else uncomfortable with my disregard. If you would please have my carriage brought around, I shall take my leave before the others arrive."

Amelia, looking crestfallen and bewildered, jumped up from the chair and began to pace the flagstone terrace, her strawberry satin evening gown rustling with every turn.

"But my dear Emmaline, you must know that Devruex is a very close friend of my husband and any number of gentlemen you are acquainted with. They have all run in the same set since they were schoolboys. My Roger, Tunbridge, Severly, Haverstone, Monteford, Westlake, even your own brother, I might add—they are all as thick as thieves. If you intend to ignore Devruex, then you will

have to avoid all his friends. I cannot imagine why you dislike him so. Has he insulted you in some way?"

Of course Emma knew that Jack was closely associated
with her brother and his friends. No matter how she had
tried to ignore news about him over the years, she had not
been able to completely avoid hearing about his exploits.

Penelope, who had remained uncharacteristically silent
during this exchange, leaned forward and said gently,
"Don't you think it's time to tell Amelia what happened?"

Emma looked from one friend to the other, and saw the
concern on Penelope's features and the anxiety on
Amelia's. Instantly, she felt horribly guilty for causing
such reactions—and completely silly for her behavior.

She threw her hands up, in a gesture of confusion and
dismay. "For a woman who has long prided herself on
self-possession I am displaying a shocking want of it at
this moment. Forgive me for discomfiting you, dear
Amelia."

"Good heavens! Penelope makes it sound as if there is
a mystery afoot. Tell me at once! What happened to make
you take Devruex into such dislike?"

Taking a sip of what was left of her sherry, Emma
leaned back in her chair as Amelia reseated herself. Penelope sent her a reassuring smile.

"'Tis a simple story, really," Emma began, striving for
a light tone. "I made a complete fool of myself over Jack
Devruex a long time ago. He quite broke my heart."

Amelia looked stunned. "Devruex? You knew him?
When? Oh, do please tell me what occurred."

Penelope nodded in agreement. "Yes, do tell us. Even I
have not heard the details for years and I believe it will do
you good, Emma."

Encouraged by their earnest, concerned expressions,
Emma took a deep breath and plunged ahead, feeling an
odd sense of relief to be able to speak of it. "I met Jack Devruex during my come-out year. I was eighteen and thought
I was so wise in the ways of the world. Almost instantly we

fancied ourselves in love," she said with a half-embarrassed smile.

"Well, who would not? Those eyes! He's terribly fascinating, and so masculine," Amelia interjected.

"Do let her speak before she changes her mind," Penelope scolded, flapping her hand at Amelia.

"I am sorry. Do please go on. I shan't interrupt again for I must hear what happened."

Looking off into the distance, Emma continued. "Jack's reputation was beyond the pale and his prospects were not impressive. My uncle Chilcrest took him into dislike and Mama thought him a certified rakehell in the making. Who could blame them for their opinion? I saw for myself how he swaggered about Town with his friends, spurs jingling, creating a stir wherever he went. I thought him terribly dashing." She was painfully aware that her tone had lost the lightness she had strived for, but she continued, urged on by the rapt expressions of her friends.

"He approached my uncle, who refused his suit out of hand. The very next day, Jack and I began to make plans to elope."

"Elope! How could you dare? Oh, I am sorry. Do continue, please." At the cross look Penelope sent her, Amelia clapped a hand over her mouth.

Emma's smile was a little wan. "So, on the designated night I sneaked out of Kelbourne Keep to run away with him, uncaring that I risked social degradation. I was frightened and tired, and I despised the idea of hurting my family, who had done nothing but indulge and love me the whole of my life."

She took a deep breath before continuing. "When I arrived, I was distressed to see him in a phaeton, of all things. Can you imagine a more inconvenient vehicle for an elopement—especially since we were so far from Scotland? Jack was so very cavalier, as if the whole thing were the merriest prank. He made jokes and it became clear that he was a little bosky. I became alarmed. Despite how much

I loved him, I could not dismiss the thought that I could be making a dreadful mistake. I do not believe that he had the foggiest notion of just what I would be sacrificing to be with him. Suddenly, all the stories my uncle had regaled me with, about how dissolute and irresponsible Jack was, came back to haunt me. I began to doubt my decision."

"That is perfectly understandable," Penelope interjected, ignoring the look Amelia sent her. "After all, you were so terribly young. So carefully brought up and sheltered. I am surprised that you had the temerity to sneak out of Kelbourne Keep in the first place."

Emma shrugged, feeling the evening air caress the tops of her shoulders. "I suppressed my doubts and we rode off in the phaeton, but he drove the wrong way. For miles he went in the opposite direction and did not even notice. On top of everything else . . . well, I panicked and bolted. As I stood on that dark road, soaking wet from the rain, tired and frightened, I realized that he must not have really loved me." She stopped abruptly, startled at the rough catch of lingering pain and sorrow in her own voice.

The three of them sat in silence for a moment until Amelia said softly, "But you were only eighteen and Devruex was not much older. Maybe he truly did love you and when you ran away . . ."

Emma shook her head as Amelia's voice trailed off. "No. I am coming to the end of my sad tale," she said, attempting a self-deprecating little laugh. "The next day, when I had calmed down, I knew my feelings for him had not changed. I waited, confident that he would come to Kelbourne Keep, sober and more serious about the action we intended to take. It never entered my love-struck little brain that he would not come back. I waited and waited like a besotted fool with my nose pressed against the windowpane. But he never came back. I did not receive so much as a note. So you see, his professed love for me was obviously not very deep or enduring. Three months later, I married Charles."

"Oh, Emma," Amelia said, her eyes full of tears and her tone full of awe. "I hardly know what to say. I never would have suspected that you had something like this in your past. Since I have known you, you have been the model of all that is poised and circumspect. This is so tragically romantic. I feel quite teary just thinking of how much this must have hurt you and I never knew. But, surely, it is behind you now?"

Spreading her hands wide, Emma said, "I do not know why his presence should throw me into such confusion. Last night, when we danced, I had every intention of behaving as if I barely recalled Lord Devruex. Instead, I behaved like a shrew. I am certain that he is gloating over the fact that I have never forgotten him. It's ridiculous to be this angry after nearly thirteen years, for heaven's sake. My life has been so busy that I have scarce given him a thought. Yet now . . ." She could not put into words the bewildering emotions that had gripped her heart since seeing Jack again.

Penelope nodded her blond head in understanding. "Yes, you organized your homes with impeccable skill and you played hostess to your husband's family and friends. After dealing with such a terrible tragedy early in your marriage, then coping with the loss of Charles, you built and directed the management of not only a school but an orphanage as well. You have also championed the rights of children working in mills in Yorkshire. And you are an accomplished harpist and gardener. Lord only knows what else I have left out of your hectic schedule."

Emma turned to look at her old friend, a puzzled frown furrowing her brow. "And what is the point of this recitation of what is on my calendar?"

Penelope sent her a look of keen understanding. "To illustrate that you have finally run out of things to occupy every moment of your time. Mind, I am not saying that you do not enjoy all those activities, but keeping so busy has held the past at bay. Don't you know, Emma," Penelope said with uncharacteristic gravity, a suspicious sheen in her large green eyes, "that in matters of love it does not signify how much time has gone by, the heart never forgets."

Chapter Eleven

"Despite your earlier trepidation, I would hazard to say that you are now enjoying yourself," Amelia said, leaning close so that Emma could hear her over the jig being played by a nearby quartet and the raucous noise coming from the other supper boxes.

Sending a quick glance to the other end of the table, Emma saw, through the flickering flames of a stout brace of candles, Devruex's profile and deep dimples. Mrs. Bruce, seated next to him, threw her head back and laughed uproariously at something he said.

Again, that inexplicable flash of anger flared within her. Taking a deep breath, she turned back to Amelia.

"I can say that I am, thanks to you." She sent Amelia an affectionate smile. "You were very adroit at making sure Devruex and I were in different coaches for the ride here."

Amelia grinned as the server refilled their goblets with potent arrack punch. "Easiest thing in the world! As it was, we needed two conveyances, and placing you at opposite ends of our supper box proved just as easy. With all this music and laughter you can hardly be expected to shout at each other across the length of the table."

"No, indeed," Emma said, "and if Mrs. Bruce keeps his attention focused upon her, I shall not have to speak more than ten words to him this evening."

This was true, for when Devruex had arrived at the Spence-Jones townhouse, looking disturbingly handsome in his dark blue jacket, he barely had time to do much more than bow and fix her with his dark, amused gaze before Amelia had whisked him off to meet the ebullient, auburn-haired Mrs. Bruce.

Roger had then presented to Emma the stout Mr. Bosworth, Mrs. Bruce's brother. Moments later, they had all left the townhouse in a merry hurry.

Mrs. Bruce's hearty laugh pulled Emma's thoughts back to her engaging dinner companions.

"And how do you like Vauxhall Gardens, Lady Fallbrook? I know you have never been here before. Does it meet your expectations?"

Emma turned to Penelope's dashing husband with a smile. "It does, sir. I could not have imagined such a place existed. The lanterns and faerie lights illuminate the promenades with such beautiful and fanciful colors that it quite chases the night away. I had no notion that the crowds would be so dense and diverse."

He sent her a mischievous look. "Did you notice the transparencies?"

Emma laughed and tapped him playfully on his arm. "Ah, I see the roguish twinkle in your eyes, Tunbridge. You must have seen the way I practically jumped when I saw that ragged hermit, only to find out on closer inspection that it was just a clever illusion," Emma said, meeting his smiling hazel eyes with her own.

Lifting his goblet he said, "A toast to you, Lady Fallbrook. And may I say that it is good to have you gracing Society again? We have missed your bright company."

"Oh, sir, no wonder Penelope never ceases to sing your praises," she said with warm affection.

To her surprised amusement, she could see a ruddy flush come to his handsome features.

"Does she?" he murmured.

Before Emma could reply, Penelope turned from her conversation with Mr. Bosworth on the other side of the table and said, "Lady Fallbrook, you must come to the Severly races next month! It absolutely cannot be missed."

Emma recalled that Grandmère had mentioned the Severly Stakes this afternoon, and that Devruex had a horse entered. Just then, the smooth, deep timbre of Devruex's laugh drew her gaze to where he, Roger, and Mrs. Bruce sat less than two yards from her in deep conversation.

"I have not had the honor of an invitation," Emma said, dragging her attention back to Penelope.

"I am sure that is only because Severly has no notion that you are in Town," the petite blonde said with a dismissive wave of her hand. "I will make sure that you receive an invitation. Although it is only an hour or so out of Town, it is much more pleasant to spend the night at Longdown."

"I thought the Severlys lived in Derbyshire." Emma had known the Duke of Severly years ago, for he and her brother, Kel, were old friends. She had not seen the duke since his marriage a couple of years ago.

"They do, but Severly purchased Longdown because of its proximity to London and the good stretch of flat land on which to run his horses," Tunbridge supplied. "The races started informally, but for the last few years it's become the most talked about meet of the Season. By a complex method of preliminary heats, five horses are entered into each of two races. The first is for fillies."

"It was terribly exciting last year," Amelia interjected. "The weather was perfect and we all drove out together and claimed a spot on the grass near the finish line. We brought picnic baskets and visited with everyone because nothing starts on time, which makes it all perfectly lovely. The Severly races have become all the crack."

"I confess myself surprised," Emma said. "I always thought Severly was quite private. It's difficult to imagine him sponsoring such an event."

At a sudden burst of nearby music, Penelope set her cup down and leaned toward Emma. "Severly has softened a bit since he's married the beautiful Celia. Tunbridge says that so many of the important races have become a bore—too crowded, too ripe for corruption. The Severly Stakes are kept small, but the side betting is enormous. The prizes are presented to the winning owners at the ball later in the evening."

"Some people," Amelia interjected, "who know they don't have a prayer of being invited, put it around long before the invitations are sent that they have obligations in Town during the Severly races."

As she smiled at the vanities of Society, Emma's attention was again caught by Mrs. Bruce's laugh, and she glanced down the table to see Devruex smiling at the auburn-haired beauty.

"It would seem that Mrs. Bruce is also enjoying herself," Amelia said, giving Emma a sideways smile.

"Is her laugh rather shrill or is it just me?" Emma was beginning to find everything about Mrs. Bruce irritating.

Amelia grinned. "I do find her a little too jolly, but Mr. Bosworth is Roger's particular friend."

At that moment, Roger, sitting on the widow's right, pushed his chair back and stood up. Smiling at his guests, he said, "Come now, we must all make haste if we are going to gain a good view of the fireworks."

Amelia rose and moved to her husband's side. "Yes, we must stay close. The crowds are terrific."

As Lord Tunbridge assisted his wife, then Emma, from their chairs, Emma glanced again at Jack. He offered Mrs. Bruce his hand to help her rise, and with a huge smile she took it, holding it for longer than was necessary.

Taking a moment to carefully adjust her heavily embroidered lilac blue shawl to drape at her elbows just so, Emma told herself sternly not to look in his direction again.

They all left the semiprivate supper box and were instantly immersed in a sea of excited merrymakers. The red-and-gold lanterns dazzled Emma's eyes and she was fascinated to see that many people wore fanciful masks and gamboled about the promenade like children around a may-pole.

She continued to weave through the crowd, finding it difficult to keep up with her friends. As warm bodies seemed to press around her, she paused to catch her breath. She had never been in such a large crowd and found it a little unnerving.

"Lady Fallbrook! I knew I could not be mistaken! It is you."

At the vaguely familiar voice, Emma whipped her head around and met a pair of smiling, warm brown eyes.

"Lord Darley!" She was quite surprised to see him, perhaps because she had hardly given him a thought since they had danced last night.

"Good evening," she said, feeling a true smile come to her lips. Even though she had practically forgotten him, she had to admit that she found his eager, admiring expression quite flattering.

"How delightful to see you, Lady Fallbrook. It is a very fine night for fireworks—if a bit crowded," he said in vast understatement.

Someone jostled him, seemingly to confirm his statement. He made a comical face and Emma laughed at his charming good nature. Glancing around, she saw that the boisterous crowd had separated her from the others, and her friends were now some distance away. "Oh, you are correct. I am here with the Spence-Joneses and the Tunbridges but we have already become separated."

"I came with Lords Trevor and Monteford and Mrs. W—er—and other friends, but I fear they are lost to me."

Emma tried to hide her smile as he flushed red at nearly making the uncouth mistake of mentioning Mrs. Willoughby to her. Glancing past Darley's shoulder, she could not mistake Devruex's broad back moving away from her. Mrs. Bruce clung to his arm, and even from here, Emma could hear her hearty laugh above the din.

"Are you well, Lady Fallbrook?"

Pulling her gaze away from Devruex, she attempted to smile at Darley. "I am fine, sir. It is just that I am unused to such crowds."

"If you will allow, I can escort you to a less crowded area of the gardens. It won't have as clear a view of the fireworks display as we have here, but it will no doubt be less crowded."

Tilting her head to the side, Emma admired the fit of his claret-colored jacket while considering his offer. She was tempted. After all, she came to London seeking what her life in Yorkshire so obviously lacked. With a last glance at Devruex's back and a sudden stubborn sense of thrill, Emma decided that Vauxhall Gardens, of all places, seemed exactly the right place for a walk with a handsome man.

Glancing back in the direction the others had gone, she spared a worried thought that Amelia and Penelope would think she'd gotten herself lost and send a search party.

Just then, she caught sight of Penelope's bright curls. Penelope turned and scanned the crowd with a slight frown. A moment later, their eyes met.

Holding Penelope's gaze, Emma tilted her head in a significant way toward Darley, hoping her friend would take her meaning.

Even from this distance, Emma could see her friend's delighted and encouraging smile. With a cheery wave, Penelope turned back to her husband.

Feeling free to be daring, Emma gave Lord Darley her most dazzling smile. "I would like that very much." Her voice sounded a little firmer than she intended.

With a winning grin, he held out his arm to her and began to lead her through the raucous throng—even passing the odd sight of a man on stilts—until the numbers began to thin. Moments later they turned through a gap between the hedgerow onto a tree-lined lane that was much less illuminated than the Grand Walk they had just left.

Lord Darley kept up a steady stream of conversation as Emma admired the firmness of the arm beneath her fingers.

The festive voices and music became a distant drone, and their feet crunching along the graveled path, with the soft sounds of birds roosting in the tall trees, brought a quite unexpected feeling of intimacy to the situation.

Suddenly, the memory of Devruex teasing her about the wagers being placed on her possible marriage to Darley made her defiantly glad that she had gone off with him.

They walked farther down the quiet path until a break in the line of trees and hedges brought them to a different view of the river.

"Here we are, Lady Fallbrook. We shall be able to see at least part of the fireworks from here." He stopped beneath a tree where a lone Chinese lantern swung from a low branch.

Gazing up at his engagingly handsome face, she wondered if he would attempt to kiss her and what she would do if he did. With a thumping heart, she decided this was preferable to watching Mrs. Bruce simpering over Devruex.

"Now this is better, is it not?" Darley asked softly.

"Much." She gazed up at him, the lantern casting a deep red glow over his broad, handsome features.

Their eyes held for a moment and he said, "Lady Fallbrook, I must tell you how honored I am that—"

To her amusement, he cleared his throat and tried again. "That is, I am above honored that you would entrust me—"

"Good evening, Lady Fallbrook."

At the sharp voice cutting through the warm night air, Emma jumped and whipped her head around to see Lord Monteford approaching them along the shadowed path. An immediate feeling of annoyance rushed through her at the unexpected interruption.

"Evening, Monteford," Darley said, and Emma could see that he also appeared unpleasantly surprised by the visitor.

Monteford, dressed in a dark evening coat with a ridiculously high collar, bowed deeply to Emma. She refused to hold her hand out for him to salute. The niggling instinct that had warned her against him last night solidified to avid dislike. "Good evening, Lord Monteford," she said coolly, determined not to be more polite than necessary.

Ignoring her slight, he turned to his friend. "Good evening, Darley. Mrs. Pennyworth is wondering where you got off to," he stated pointedly.

Emma did not care who Mrs. Pennyworth was, and she did not like Lord Monteford's scolding tone of voice. She sent an encouraging look to Darley, fully expecting him to give Monteford a proper set-down for his barely veiled impertinence.

Instead, to her surprise, Darley stood there looking down, shifting his weight from foot to foot.

"So shall we escort Lady Fallbrook back to the fireworks?" Monteford said with a sharp look to Darley.

Lord Darley, clearly uncomfortable, frowned and said, "Er, certainly, Monteford."

Emma shot Lord Darley a look of exasperation, disappointed that he would allow Monteford to bully him this way. She was certainly not going to stand for this insufferable cheek from Lord Monteford another moment.

Sending him a scathing look of contempt, Emma said, "Such attentions are certainly not necessary, my lord. I am perfectly capable of finding my way. Good evening," she finished abruptly and turned away.

"Oh! Please permit me to escort you back, Lady Fallbrook," Darley called.

Already striding down the graveled pathway, she tossed over her shoulder, "There is no need," and kept walking, aware that they were following her.

A feeling of deep disappointment hit her hard. She would certainly be striking Lord Darley off her list of potential lovers and would definitely not be driving with him in the park tomorrow. She had no interest in someone so unwilling to stand up to his overconfident friend.

She heard Monteford say, "Darley, why don't you toddle

along? Lady Fallbrook may trust me to make sure she returns unmolested."

Glancing back, she paused when she saw Darley's abashed expression. Pressing his lips together, he made a shallow, quick bow and muttered, "Good evening, Lady Fallbrook," and walked quickly past her down the lane.

Staring after him and gritting her teeth in annoyance, Emma hitched up her shawl and continued marching up the path, back toward the main promenade.

"Lady Fallbrook, allow me to offer you my arm."

Insulted beyond speech, Emma turned her head to see that Lord Monteford had caught up with her. His unctuous smile caused a repulsed shiver to ripple through her body.

"No, thank you, Lord Monteford. I have no desire for your company," she said coldly and resumed walking. She could no longer see Lord Darley.

An instant later, a hard grip on her arm abruptly halted her steps. The unwanted contact startled her to the point that she stared at his fingers gripping her flesh for a moment before looking up at him. A searing anger brought heat to her cheeks. No one had ever touched her person so roughly, not even Charles.

"Now we cannot have this, Lady Fallbrook," he said in a patient tone. "After your bold glances at the theatre and last night, I would not have expected such coyness from you."

Unable to think clearly for a moment, she shook off his grip and continued to stare at him. "In the face of such insufferable presumption I hardly know what to say."

"Come now," he said with a chuckle and took a step closer, "there really is no need for these artful displays of shyness, my lady. We both know what is between us. I will not think less of you for your boldness. Unless this is a hint that you would prefer that I sweep you off your feet. Actually, you impress me as a woman who would enjoy such a display of my passion."

Emma closed her mouth, for she knew that she must have been gaping at him like a caught trout.

"You know, I do not believe that I have ever met anyone with less reason to be so arrogant. You will cease to importune me, sir." Turning on her heel, she took quick steps to place as much space between them as possible.

"Is it possible that you mistake my intentions?" she heard him say as he came up behind her.

She walked faster. "I do not give a fig what your intentions are, sir."

"Oh, but I believe you will when you learn that they are completely *honorable*, my lady," he said as he practically trotted alongside of her.

This pronouncement slowed her pace and she almost laughed at the ridiculousness of this scene.

"You must be mad! I do not even know you. If you think I will feel any different because of your professed honorable intentions, you are seriously misguided."

Lord Monteford had the gall to look affronted. This time, when she felt his harsh grip on her arm, she was prepared.

Spinning around, she jerked her arm down and then kicked his leg as hard as she could. The impact caused her toes to sting through her soft leather slippers. When he landed on his backside with a thud she looked down at him in complete shock, surprised that her hastily planned defense had been so successful.

Gathering her trailing shawl, she watched his stunned face and thought that this sort of thing was not at all what she had in mind when she had decided to come to London for some excitement.

He quickly scrambled to his feet, and she turned to run from him, but his speed was such that he was in front of her before she could take more than a few strides.

"Not so fast, my lady. You will pay for this insult."

For the first time, she felt a frisson of fear. Despite the fact that only some trees and hedges separated her from thousands of people, she knew by the harsh frown distorting his handsome features that he did not intend to let her go so easily.

Refusing to show any of her trepidation, she stared up at him defiantly, prepared to defend her honor in any way she could.

"No, Monteford, it will be you who pays. I suggest you name your second."

At the harshly spoken words, Emma whipped around and gasped in surprise to see Devruex approaching, some ten steps away. His almost casually spoken words shocked her as much as his unexpected presence. Even in the inadequate light, she could see the cold fury stamped upon his features.

Chapter Twelve

Stunned by Jack's words, Emma felt incapable of finding her voice. Shifting her gaze back to Monteford, she saw that he looked shocked as well.

"Are you challenging me, Devruex? But this is too droll. You mistake the situation, my friend. Lady Fallbrook and I were just indulging in a bit of high spirits," Monteford said in a jovial tone of voice, completely unlike the tone he had used toward her a moment ago.

Sorely tempted to kick him again, Emma opened her mouth to call him a liar, but Devruex spoke first.

"I mistake nothing. And you are most unwise to add insult upon insult. Swords or pistols?"

At the implacable tone in Devruex's voice, Emma felt even more alarmed than she had a moment ago. This absurd scene had gone far enough and she felt the immediate need to intervene. "Stop this nonsense! Would the two of you stop speaking as if I am not standing right here?"

Devruex shifted his angry gaze to her. "Emmaline, if you think I am going to let him get away with this, you are terribly mistaken."

She started to argue when a shrill voice suddenly cut through the air and they all turned to see Mrs. Willoughby rushing toward them in a flurry of plum silk skirts. "You must not duel! You cannot!"

She stopped in front of Devruex, her beautiful face marred by an outraged scowl.

"This is not fair! I will not stand for this! If there is going to be a duel fought then it must be over me! What will everyone think? It is not fair, I say." She turned to Monteford and stamped her feet. "Monteford, you shall break my heart! After everything I have given you, how dare you insult me in this manner. No! It will not be so! I want a duel fought over me! Lady Fallbrook, it is most unfair of you to steal my thunder like this."

Struck speechless by such outrageous behavior, Emma fought back an unexpected wave of laughter. Glancing over at Devruex, she saw the muscle in his jaw working and there was a suspicious glint in his eyes. He turned his head and for an instant their eyes met in shared amusement.

Marveling at the vain audacity of Monteford's mistress, Emma shook her head in amazement. "My dear Mrs. Willoughby, I have to say that your inappropriate forwardness is as impressive as Lord Monteford's. The two of you are indeed well suited."

Mrs. Willoughby closed her mouth midscold and her scowl cleared. For a moment she looked flattered.

Next to her, Devruex's cough sounded suspiciously like a laugh, but Emma kept her gaze on Mrs. Willoughby.

But at Monteford's guffaw, Mrs. Willoughby's face changed again in a flash. "There you go again! How do you do it? You just insulted me, yet your tone is as if you were inviting me to take tea."

Shrugging, Emma said, "I would apologize, but I find you terribly vexing."

"Ha! Me vexing? You are not so different from me, Miss High-and-Mighty Lady Fallbrook. I suspect that you would behave exactly as I am, were I trying to steal Devruex from you. Looking back, I now suspect that Devruex's arrival was not a coincidence this morning. Really, it is too unsporting of you to want both of them."

"Both! Good Lord, I certainly do not want either of them."

"That's rather lowering to a gent's address," Devruex said, his deep voice filled with languid amusement.

Emma saw the glint in his dark eyes and felt mortified at her presumption. "That is—er—what I meant to say was that Lord Devruex and I do not want each other—" She stopped, realizing how foolish she must sound.

"Speak for yourself, my lady."

At this rejoinder, Emma's gaze flew back to Devruex's, and the expression in his eyes had her heart thumping anew.

"What's this? Have you been trying to steal a march on me, Devruex? Maybe I will meet you at dawn, at that." Monteford's tone was more bluster than threat.

"No! Monteford," Mrs. Willoughby shrieked, "you must think of my reputation! How could I ever face anyone again if you duel over another woman? You shall break my heart, I swear."

"Mrs. Willoughby, no one is going to fight a duel," Emma said sternly. "You are a most curious creature. Why you would find a duel fought over you flattering baffles me. I find the very suggestion insulting as well as uncivilized." She lobbed a pointed look at Devruex. It was imperative that this talk of duels stop. Why, Grandmère would have apoplexy if such a thing reached her ears, Emma thought in horror.

Devruex met her gaze squarely, but his expression didn't change.

Mrs. Willoughby gave a petulant shrug. "I am sure that is easy for you to say. I probably should not have spoken so to you, but I have always let my temper run away with me. Something I am sure you know nothing about as you are the *perfectly perfect* Lady Fallbrook," Mrs. Willoughby said scornfully.

"You would not have thought so a few minutes ago," Monteford muttered as he reached down to rub his leg.

Mrs. Willoughby turned to him and put her hands on her hips. "Monteford, come away with me at once! I am livid! You shall not fight a duel with Lord Devruex over another woman. If you do not come at once you shall force me to something desperate—like—like sending a note to your mother. Neither one of you would like that, I'd wager."

Monteford raised an index finger and pointed it an inch away from Mrs. Willoughby's face. "Now you are over-stepping yourself, Sally. You should not have followed me. You know I always insist upon the distinction of rank being preserved. Go back to our party at once."

"I shall not! You cannot make me!"

Emma cringed as Mrs. Willoughby's voice reached an entirely new octave.

At that moment, Devruex stepped forward and offered Emma his arm. "May I escort you back, Lady Fallbrook? I believe the fireworks have come to an end," Devruex said with dry amusement.

Hesitating for an instant, Emma looked into his devilish black gaze. Feeling her heart lurch she took his arm. "Why, thank you, Lord Devruex. I believe there have been enough fireworks for one evening."

Chapter Thirteen

A s they set off down the path at an elegant pace, Emma
hardly knew what to say and struggled with the inelegant urge to giggle as she heard Mrs. Willoughby's continued shrieks behind her.

Casting a quick glance at Jack's striking profile, she
thought it ironic that he should be the one to come to her
rescue.

Striving for some normalcy, she said, "Thank you for
arriving when you did, Lord Devruex."

"Think nothing of it, Lady Fallbrook. If I had not happened upon you, Mrs. Willoughby was certainly not far
behind."

Startled into a laugh by his dry humor, Emma looked
up at him again. A moment later, her gaze strayed to his
slight smile.

Being so close to him brought to mind another balmy
night, long ago, when they had daringly sneaked out of a
ballroom to a secluded garden. There, they had shared
their first kiss beneath a vine-covered arbor. It had been an
intensely passionate kiss that had confirmed to her that
their love was eternal. How young and foolish she had
been, she thought with a flare of anger.

Nevertheless, as she walked with him now along the
darkened path, his body brushing against her side, that
kiss did not seem so long ago. Suddenly she felt a deep,
hot anger rising from the pit of her stomach.

Tilting her head up, she sent him a look full of speculation. "How did you come upon us?" she asked, not car-
ing that her tone had an edge.

He looked down, and his slight smile did not waver as
he cocked a black brow at her. "I would have sworn that
only a few moments ago you were pleased to see me. Now
I have the opposite impression."

"That is not an answer, sir."

His black gaze flickered over her and her heart began
to pound again.

He shrugged. "I saw you walking with Darley. A moment later I watched Monteford follow. I did not think you
were expecting him. And you know what a curious fellow
I can be."

Feeling helpless in the face of her own spiraling emotions, Emma said nothing.

Not far away, stringed instruments filled the air with a
waltz. Emma's every sense felt keenly aware of the tall,
muscular body next to hers and she hoped she betrayed no
outward signs of her distress. She had already exposed too
many of her emotions to him.

"So is Darley still your favorite?"

At the look she sent him, he laughed richly. "I thought not."

Another question occurred to her and she could not resist asking, "You were not really serious when you challenged Lord Monteford to a duel, were you?"

His smile faded completely away. "Of course I was."

"Why?" Dueling was not only illegal, but she had un-
derstood that Monteford and Devruex were friends.

He looked down at her, his dark eyes roving over her
features, but he did not answer.

She had to look away, and watched her feet as they
continued along the graveled path. "Well, I am just glad
it's over," she said.

"I do not believe that you need be concerned that Monteford will annoy you again."

"Oh, I'm not." And she meant it. The only things concerning her were the disturbing emotions stirring within her at his nearness. Being this close to him was a torment that she could neither fully understand nor dismiss.

"That's right. I forgot for a moment that you had come to London looking for adventure," he said as they walked beneath the glow of a low hanging lantern.

Bristling at the teasing challenge in his voice, she said, "I still am. I will just have to try again and hope for better luck next time."

He stopped abruptly and she, perforce, stopped as well and looked up at him in surprise. Her heart fluttered at the expression of intensity in his eyes.

As he faced her, his features—all shadows and planes—revealed nothing of his thoughts. Anger swelled within her and she clenched her fingers into fists.

Once upon a time she had believed that they would always be attuned to each other's every feeling. During that fleeting spring, a shared glance was all they needed to understand every bit of longing and laughter and passion the other felt. Looking at the enigmatic man before her, she could not imagine how they ever shared that kind of intimacy.

His gaze had not left her face. "Then Monteford's interruption must be doubly vexing."

She sensed a sharpness beneath the amusement lacing his tone. Crossing her arms over her chest, she said, "How so?"

"He not only insulted you, but prevented you from enjoying the moonlight with Darley."

"Yes, that was certainly more annoying than forcing his honorable intentions upon me."

"The evening does not have to be a complete loss."

She watched him with narrowed eyes, wondering what he was about. "Oh?"

"You could continue to walk in the moonlight with me."

At the hint of challenge in his tone, her heart began to race and the temptation to pretend the past no longer mattered almost made her take his arm again. But her finely developed sense of self-protection burst to the surface.

"No, thank you. If I did, then the evening really would be a loss." As soon as the words left her lips, she desperately wished them back. What was wrong with her? It was completely out of her character to be so cutting.

"You are a most curious creature," he said. "Tell me why you are so angry."

"I told you, I am not—"

He stepped closer and she had to tilt her chin up to look at him, but she did not step back.

"It's far too late to pretend otherwise, Emmaline."

In the half-light beneath the trees, his deep voice rumbled over her, and old familiar feelings swirled through her. She could not find her voice to save her life.

He moved imperceptibly closer, but she still did not move. She watched his gaze travel down to her mouth and her heart began to hammer.

He is going to kiss me, came the breathless realization. As his head lowered, and with a dizzying feeling of anticipation, she lifted her chin ever so slightly. Just as she felt his warm breath on her lips she closed her eyes and in the next instant he pulled her against his chest.

Unthinking, she responded to the warm, firm pressure of his lips as if her will were no longer her own. Putting her hands on his hard chest, she felt his heart beating beneath her fingers before sliding her arms around his neck.

She shivered as his hands caressed her back through the thin material of her gown and pulled her closer. Her hand settled on the smooth, warm nape of his neck and her pliant body seemed to meld into the hard lines of his as the kiss deepened.

With her other hand, she pushed aside her shawl so that she could press against him even closer. His lips moved against hers more urgently and at the rumble of his groan, the passion his touch ignited flared even higher.

Parting her lips at the insistent tug of his mouth, she felt his need and, touching her tongue to his, was instantly lost to their magic.

He kissed her again and again until her hands bit into his back to keep her knees, weak with need, from collapsing.

For thirteen years she hadn't felt his touch, had nearly forgotten the pleasurable, aching hunger that shot through her with renewed intensity.

Because of him, the hazy thought surfaced through the passion, she had never known what life could have been like.

All the years, all the sad, dull, duty-filled years that had unfolded between their last kiss and this moment tumbled down upon her with suffocating force.

Suddenly, it became utterly clear why his presence stirred up such a searing anger within her.

If only he had not arrived the night of their intended elopement half foxed and gotten them lost, this feeling of passion, and desire, could have been hers for the last thirteen years.

While the dreams of her youth had slipped away, while tragedy scarred her heart, while Charles had worn her down with his petty tyranny—she had been missing *this*.

His lips slid across her cheek, to her ear. "Emmaline."

The hungry, rough sound of his voice speaking her name heightened her heartbreaking sense of loss. She whispered, "Oh, how I hate you."

If it were possible, his arms tightened even more around her pliant body. Emma closed her eyes and breathed in the warm, smoky scent of him.

"You are faced with quite the dilemma," he finally said, his lips still against her ear.

Opening her passion heavy lids, she pulled back and met his gaze. "Dilemma?"

"You may hate me, but, my dear Lady Fallbrook, you want me just as much."

Chapter Fourteen

At the break of dawn, Jack boarded his traveling coach and headed for Woodhouse, his small estate less than two hours beyond London.

He had purchased the hundred-acre property a few years ago because of its excellent state of repair and the size of its mews and stable yard. Its convenient proximity to London and Newmarket was an added bonus.

The house itself had been the least of his considerations when he had first toured the property. However, after the purchase, he discovered it to be as perfectly proportioned and charming as a jewel box.

As his carriage turned up the well-manicured, curving drive he felt a sense of pride.

During the dark years right after Emma had left him, the only thing that had sustained him was the fierce need to overcome his penury and somehow restore his family's good name—as well as its coffers.

It had been difficult, but he had sold a few more family heirlooms and, on the advice of trusted friends, had invested the money in a venture in the West Indies. It had seemed like a miracle when his investment paid off handsomely.

Through more careful investing and management—including ambitious improvements to his farms—his fortunes had turned dramatically.

After working to put things right at Kingsmount, he had

been able to purchase Woodhouse and begin to actively pursue his desire to breed blood horses. And he had managed to do it without any financial difficulty.

Now, several years later, he was an extremely wealthy man, but had not forgotten what it had been like to struggle.

Woodhouse reminded him of how sweet it felt to overcome those obstacles. Even though the manor was only one-fifth the size of Kingsmount, he had grown to feel very much at home in the picturesque place.

Unfortunately, that was not the case this morning, he thought some hours later as he made his way toward the mews.

Usually, he thrived in the hivelike atmosphere of his stud farm. But as he strode past stable boys busily going about their chores, the usual solace he found was patently missing.

In the yard, Caleb, his head trainer, was in the process of giving Tommy—who was going to ride Circes in the Severly Stakes—instructions.

"Now take her for a run, but don't be giving her her head too soon," Caleb told the wiry jockey. "Just get her good and warm. Then we'll run her against Persephone 'cause she's the only one who can keep up with our Circes."

Jack approached and leaned his forearms atop the fence as Tommy urged the chestnut filly into an easy trot. Doffing his cap as he went by his master, Tommy led the horse out of the stable yard.

Devruex swept his gaze over the filly as she pranced in the same high-spirited way that had caught his attention mere weeks after her birth.

The Duke of Richmond and Squire Watt—both men renowned for their keen judgment of horseflesh—had expressed the opinion that the filly was too high-strung to have the heart of a champion.

But Jack had known different. Beneath her skittish surface, Circes was fearless.

Just like Emmaline, he thought, recalling how she had

knocked Monteford on his arse and refused to back down from his threats. Despite his continued desire to flatten Monteford he could not help smiling at the memory.

Caleb finally noticed him leaning on the wood railing of the fence. A grin split his grizzled features as he trotted over.

"Good morning, Caleb. Everything looks in fine form," Devruex called.

The groom gave a quick bow of appreciation and said, "We wasn't expectin' your lordship this week, or I would have held up Tommy so you could take Circes out yourself this fine morning."

He glanced back to see Circes and Tommy trotting off into the lush green parkland beyond the stable yard. "That's all right. I was thinking it might be best if Tommy is the only one to ride Circes until after the race."

Caleb rubbed his chin and nodded. "I'll tell the rest of the boys, sir."

"What else has been happening?" Devruex asked.

As the trainer—who liked nothing better than to go over every detail of every horse the baron owned—launched into a long monologue, Jack's thoughts instantly began to wander.

Nodding occasionally, Jack allowed the groom's gravelly voice to roll over him as the events of last night replayed in his mind.

Emmaline Fallbrook was the most maddening woman he had ever met. This thought returned for the countless time since a pack of drunken dandies, coming down the dark walk and singing at the tops of their lungs, had forced them to separate.

Jack had led her back to the promenade and their friends without a word and had not had a chance to speak to her again. To his great annoyance, they had left the gardens in different coaches.

Now, standing in familiar surroundings in the bright morning light, he found it difficult to comprehend how much she had changed in the last thirteen years. At the age of eighteen she had been bright as quicksilver and expressively volatile. She had delighted him, as well as the beau monde, with her artless, direct manner.

Her youthful prettiness had grown into a beauty and elegance that filled him with admiration, desire, and deep regret.

As they walked together in the balmy night air, he had struggled to tamp down the passion spreading throughout his body.

Thirteen years had passed and all she had to do was turn those amazing sea blue eyes toward him and he followed her like a besotted boy, he thought with sharp self-disgust.

However, he found her sophisticated façade almost impossible to read, which was why her passionate response to his kiss had taken him by complete—and pleasurable—surprise.

Lost in the unexpected intensity of their kiss, he had been on the verge of leading her out of the gardens to a hackney carriage when her softly spoken words had him doubting his hearing.

Oh, how I hate you. The words reverberated through him even now. The fierce sadness in her voice had been unmistakable—but so had the desire in her touch.

What right had she to hate him? he thought with a flash of long suppressed anger. She had left him—a boy with little to offer except ambition, to marry the wealthy, socially accepted Charles Fallbrook.

By her vehemence, one would think that *he* had left *her* on the side of that dark road. Running his fingers through his hair, he gritted his teeth against the same onslaught of emotion that had forced him from London this morning.

But beneath the scar of this old wound, embarrassment over his actions that night surfaced once again. He had been more than foolish to think that eloping in a high-perch phaeton could work. And drinking to bolster his courage and going the wrong way had not helped matters. But still, he had been so confident of her love that it had torn his heart out that she could leave him over what he considered such trivial matters. He could not have been more mistaken.

"Your lordship does not think that is the right way to go about it?"

At the concern in Caleb's voice Jack quickly smoothed his expression. "No, no, you are exactly right," he said quickly, without having a clue as to what the horse trainer just said.

Sensing that Caleb was winding down, Jack pulled his thoughts from the maddening Emmaline.

He could not deny that he was willing to go along with whatever game she was playing. But he intended to step very carefully, for he would be damned if he was going to be a fool again.

Chapter Fifteen

"I am shocked, truly shocked at Lord Monteford's behavior," Amelia said, her soft blue eyes wide with concern.

"I am more shocked by Darley's behavior," Penelope rejoined with a tone of disgust. "I would never have guessed that he was so pusillanimous."

Emma sent a wry smile to her friends as the three of them sat in her grandmother's beautifully appointed salon. "If you mean spineless and craven, I agree. But I am not shocked, just disgusted—with both of them."

Penelope and Amelia had arrived a half an hour ago, two elegant inquisitors demanding to know what had occurred last night at Vauxhall Gardens. They had not failed to notice that she had gone off with Lord Darley and returned with Lord Devruex.

Earlier, Emma had pled fatigue when Grandmère had invited her on one of her afternoon excursions. Emma knew her friends well and was expecting them, so she did not want to be out when they called.

"You do look a little tired, my dear," Grandmère had said. "Rest this afternoon and we shall have a quiet evening at home. Who would have thought that I would have more stamina than you for the social whirl?" With an impish smile the beautiful old lady had swept out of the house.

Once settled in chairs around the tea tray—and practically before the ladies had removed their bonnets—Emma had relayed almost all the details of her experiences with

Lords Darley, Monteford, and Devruex, and the fatuous Mrs. Willoughby.

That is, all the details except for the kiss with Devruex. Her thoughts about him and her passionate response were still too troubling to share.

"Thank goodness Devruex arrived when he did."

Amelia's comment brought Emma's attention back to her friends. "Yes" was all the reply she trusted herself to make about Jack. "But I am wretchedly disappointed. Now that I shall be giving the cut sublime to Darley and Monteford, I shall have to start my search all over again for an interesting gentleman."

Amelia smiled broadly over her teacup. "That will not be difficult for you. You have already captured the attention of some of the most elusive blades in Town. I cannot wait for you to fall in love. Won't it be lovely to have a wedding?"

Sitting bolt upright, Emma waved her hands vigorously to dismiss Amelia's words. "I have no objection to falling in love, but I certainly won't be getting married." The very thought of it gave her a shiver of revulsion.

Amelia's expression was one of complete dismay, and she sent a questioning look to Penelope. The petite blonde shrugged her shoulders in resignation, for she knew very well Emma's opinions on marriage.

Setting her cup on the little table next to her chair, Amelia frowned at Emma and said, "What is the point of falling in love if you don't want to marry?"

Nonplussed at her friend's artless question, Emma was suddenly gripped by helpless laughter.

Penelope joined her while Amelia looked on in growing frustration. "What is it that you two find so funny?" she demanded.

Wiping her eyes, Penelope said through her laughter, "I swear, Amelia, I know you are only a few years younger than me and Emma, but your naïveté can be so disarming."

"I was asking a serious question." Amelia's tone sounded a little affronted.

Struggling to regain her composure, Emma reached over and placed her hand affectionately on Amelia's arm. "Forgive us for laughing, dear Amelia. It is a good question and I think you are blessed to see the world the way you do. But I have not been so lucky in love. I shall never marry again, thank goodness."

"But why? Marriage is wonderful! I know you have suffered greatly in the past, but you can love again. I know you can."

Emma shrugged and spread her hands. "I have said that I am perfectly open to the idea of falling in love. In fact, I have been considering the notion of taking a lover if the right gentleman plays his hand very carefully." She refused to examine why the vision of devilish black eyes came instantly to mind at this bold declaration.

Amelia gasped. "Emma! I am shocked!"

Penelope said at the same time, "Oh, how delicious! I suspected as much."

"Are you being serious?" Amelia asked. "I can hardly believe you are not hoaxing me to get a reaction."

At the confusion and dismay in Amelia's eyes, the smile faded from Emma's lips. She realized that she must indeed seem strange to someone like Amelia and wanted to try to make her friend understand.

"I know most women are taught that any husband is preferable to no husband," Emma began in a solemn tone. "However, I do not subscribe to that belief. Never again will I give a man the right to control every aspect of my life. It is the rare man that has a strong enough character not to take advantage of a woman's frailer body and lack of personhood in the eyes of the law. You and Penelope are truly fortunate. Your husbands have always impressed me as being truly sensible of the risks and sacrifices a woman makes in giving her hand in marriage."

Penelope made no comment and Amelia, who had been listening intently, nodded slowly.

"You give me much to think about, Emma," Amelia said. "I have never looked at marriage in this way. I cannot deny that you make a good argument. It would indeed be frightening to be wed to someone unworthy. But I know, because of my marriage to my darling Roger, that where there is true love, there is respect and protectiveness. Roger would never cause me to regret entrusting myself to him."

At the quiet confidence in Amelia's voice, Emma felt a lump forming in her throat and she could not speak over the threatening tears.

"You truly are blessed among women," Penelope said softly across the tea table.

"But, Pen, don't you love Tunbridge?" Amelia looked as if someone just told her that fairies don't exist.

Emma shifted her curious gaze to Penelope to see a bright blush coming to her cheeks.

"Well . . . Tunbridge and I hold each other in great affection," she said, suddenly finding her teacup of great interest.

Amelia's eyes grew wide. "Hold each other in great affection! I thought you adored each other! I thought . . ." Her voice trailed off, her expression full of confusion and dismay.

Penelope fussed with the lace on the front panel of her yellow afternoon gown. "It is difficult to explain. Tunbridge and I are quite content with each other, but we have never expressed ourselves in such terms."

"But I would have sworn that you loved him," Amelia spluttered again.

Emma could see that poor Penelope was blushing so deeply she resembled a strawberry, and from Amelia's earnest expression, it looked as if her romantic nature would not let her drop the subject.

"Can you not see that she does, you goose?" Emma interjected before Amelia could embarrass Penelope further.

But Amelia could not be stopped. "I just cannot believe what I am hearing. I am sure Tunbridge—"

"Enough!" Penelope said, putting her cup back in its saucer with a clatter. "I refuse to speak of this anymore. It is an awful thing to be in love with one's husband."

"No, it's not!" Amelia cried, looking askance at the pretty blonde.

"Well, it is if your husband does not love you in return," Penelope said in a flat, sad voice.

"But Tunbridge dotes on you!" said Amelia. "He indulges your every whim, laughs at your scrapes, and showers you with the most stunning jewels."

Penelope made an impatient noise. "Well, of course he gives me jewels. Tunbridge has always been attentive to these gentlemanly details. How else would the world know of the respect and appreciation he feels for me? But jewels are not the same as love."

"Oh," Amelia said with dawning comprehension.

"Enough about the state of my marriage," Penelope said briskly. "I wish to get back to Emma's dilemma. You say you'll have to start over in your quest for an interesting gentleman?"

"Yes," Emma said, willing to aid Penelope in changing the subject to a less painful one. "I shall start my hunt at the Litchfield ball next week."

Penelope crossed her hands in her lap. "What about Devruex? I know your history is painful, but it was so long ago. There is not an unmarried woman—and any number of married ones—who would not be thrilled to indulge in a serious flirtation with him."

"Oh, I agree!" Amelia said eagerly. "Just look at the way he challenged Monteford over insulting you. I vow I do not know how you could resist him."

Emma could not think of a reply, for she was beginning to suspect that resisting him would not be as easy as she had at first thought.

Penelope picked up another delicate biscuit from the

tray. "Yes, Emma, how can you resist the devilishly attractive Lord Devruex?"

Emma lowered her eyes from the gentle, yet keenly perceptive green gaze of her old friend. "Because I am not interested in him," she said with more defiance than she felt.

Instantly, the memory of his strong hands pulling her against his hard body assailed her still bewildered senses. Why did her body betray her when her intellect told her that she would be ten times the fool if she allowed herself to fall under his charms again?

Penelope's knowing chuckle showed her disbelief. "Emma, I saw your face last night. You are quite practiced at concealing your emotions, but I have known you for a very long time. You may be a lot of things, but uninterested in Devruex is not one of them."

Emma wanted more than anything to deny her friend's words, but her natural honesty prevented her from doing so. Leaning back in the damask covered chair, she sighed heavily.

"I cannot deny that Devruex is an exceedingly attractive man, but I would be a fool to become involved with him again."

"But why?" Amelia asked earnestly. "It would be so terribly romantic to fall in love again with your first love."

"Absolutely not!" Emma felt a growing alarm at the trend of this conversation.

"Why not?" Penelope asked. "Amelia makes a wonderful point. You have said that you came to London seeking a bit of excitement. And, my dear, it does not get much more exciting than Jack Devruex."

Emma looked from one encouraging expression to the other, hardly believing what she was hearing. "And that is exactly why I intend to do my very best to avoid him from this moment on. I have had enough excitement from Lord Devruex for a lifetime."

Chapter Sixteen

The day before the Litchfield ball found Emma and her grandmother spending the afternoon reading and writing letters in the sun-filled sitting room that faced the back garden.

Emma appreciated the relaxed atmosphere and the breeze wafting in from the open casement windows. It was a welcome change from the previous week, which had been a whirlwind of activity.

The dowager had proudly taken her granddaughter to dinners, musical evenings, and routs. Emma enjoyed herself, but she did find it rather odd that no matter what crowded room they entered, she never once encountered Jack Devruex.

She told herself that she should be relieved, but yet she found herself looking for him every time she left her grandmother's townhouse.

"Emmaline, my dear, I am going to ask you to indulge an old lady's sensibilities."

Her grandmother's words pulled her from her reverie, and gratefully pushing aside thoughts of Jack, she smiled at the dowager, who looked the picture of regal leisure reposing on the sofa in a gauzy afternoon gown of azure blue.

"I shall certainly do my best, Grandmère."

"You must tell me if you are happy you have come to London."

The real concern in her tone surprised Emma. Quickly, she reviewed her behavior this past week, hoping she had done nothing to make her grandmother believe she regretted leaving Yorkshire.

She did not want to answer too quickly, lest her sharp-as-a-tack grandmother believe she was only trying to appease her. It took a moment to formulate a response she felt would reassure her.

"The Season, so far, has not been at all what I expected it to be. However, I am very glad that we are spending time together. I wish I had not taken so many years to accept your invitation. Attending plays and parties with you has been a delight."

To Emma's relief, the slight crease between her grandmother's brows cleared. "I daresay being admired and pursued by handsome young blades is not such a chore either."

Emma laughed, and just then Simms, the elegant butler, entered the room, carrying a salver with a stack of letters. A footman followed, carrying a massive bouquet of flowers of every sort. Pink cabbage roses, white lilies, yellow tulips, and purple larkspur filled the room with lovely fragrance and color.

As the footman set the vase on a low table next to her grandmother's chair, Emma's heart began to beat rapidly. Could Jack finally be acknowledging their kiss with this gorgeous floral tribute?

As soon as the thought fully formed, she dismissed it and chided herself for being so foolish. She wanted to forget that kiss, she reminded herself for the thousandth time.

Simms set the tray of letters next to the bouquet and bowed. "The post was a bit late today, your grace. Is there anything you require?"

"No, thank you, Simms. We shall dine at the usual time this evening."

"Very good, your grace." With another bow he and the footman left the room.

As soon as the door closed behind him, Grandmère said, "There must be a note nestled among those perfect blooms."

Emma rose and crossed to the table. A moment later she pulled an ivory parchment card, folded and sealed with a wafer of green wax, from the delicate petals.

Standing by the table in front of the window, she rubbed a fingernail between the edge of parchment and the seal and unfolded the note.

My heart shall not rest until you have forgiven me.
                                                Monteford

"I can see by your expression that it must be from Lord Monteford again," Grandmère said with a chuckle.

"Yes. How very tiresome he is," Emma replied, handing her the note. "I would have thought that he would have given up by now."

Grandmère read the note and with a sniff set it aside. "Not to insult your very obvious charms, but I hear that Monteford is fishing for a bride with deep pockets. He has been making not so discreet inquiries about several young ladies with impressive dowries. I have it on good authority that the earl has cut him off until he comes up to scratch with a suitable wife. Evidently, he is not going to give up on you until he secures someone else."

A bright smile came to Emma's face. "Indeed? He's been cut off? I am surprised we cannot hear Mrs. Willoughby's shrieks from here."

Grandmère laughed and Emma picked up the stack of letters. Sorting through them, she found several addressed to her.

"Ah, another letter from Mama," she said happily, pulling it from the pile and returning to her chair.

"You must tell me how she fares in Brighton," Grandmère said politely, sorting through her own pile of correspondence.

Settling back in the comfortable chair, Emma opened the letter and read quickly.

Dear Emmaline,

You will forgive me for dispensing with the pleasantries, but I must be direct with you. I have just received the most distressing news that you are making yourself an object of gossip in Town.

I cannot imagine what my mother-in-law must be thinking to allow such a thing.

But what is worse, and I beg you to deny it immediately, is that your name has been connected to Lord Devruex's. It cannot be so! Your uncle and I are quite alarmed, but are praying that the reports have been distorted.

Need I remind you that your behavior could reflect poorly upon your brother, whose plans for a political career must be carefully nurtured?

Lord Devruex, though I hear that he has redeemed himself somewhat over the years, is not the sort of man you should be seen associating with. I am surprised at you, Emma. After the scandal that was thankfully avoided in your youth, I would have expected you to be more circumspect.

I do hate being harsh but I am left with no choice. Please write to me immediately and put my mind to rest. If it is just idle gossip, I apologize for the harsh tone of this letter.

Your Loving Mama

Emma read the letter again, shaken by the accusing tone lacing every black pen stroke.

"Does your mother send you bad news, my love? You look quite upset."

Hardly knowing what to think, let alone what to say, Emma rose from the settee. She handed the letter to her grandmother's outstretched fingers before moving to the window to gaze out at the sunny garden.

Silence reigned for a moment as her grandmother read the short letter.

"Humph."

Emma turned from the window to see the anger sparking in her grandmother's eyes. Taking a deep breath, she tried to calm her own vexation.

"Sometimes Mama forgets that I have long been out of the schoolroom. However, I am sure it would be distressing to hear such gossip about me. She is so set on Kel taking his place in government affairs that she has grown terribly cautious."

"Stuff and nonsense," Grandmère said sharply. "It is only your mother's provincial sense of morals that has her worried about the gossip. None of the people in my set pay such things any mind."

Emma's brows rose in query. "So you have heard gossip about me and Lord Devruex?"

This really was too awful, she thought, putting a hand to her forehead. Good Lord, gossip about her and Devruex had reached Brighton! She felt hot with embarrassment, recalling how easily just anyone could have come upon them as they kissed in Vauxhall Gardens.

"Everything you do causes talk, my dear," Grandmère said, "but only in the most delightful way. No one speaks of that dreadful Mrs. Willoughby anymore. It is so much more charming for everyone to gossip about you. Despite what your dreadful mother says."

Emma tried to hide her laughter by saying, "Well, that's all very nice, Grandmère, but I do wish that you would not speak of Mama that way."

"Bah!" Grandmère said, waving the letter in disgust. "Your mother and I have never got on well, and we never shall. However"—her face cleared and her tone became thoughtful—"this letter provides me with an opening to speak with you about something that has long been on my mind."

"Goodness, you sound so serious," Emma said lightly as she moved back to the chair next to the couch. She welcomed anything that would change the subject from Jack.

"Yes, I am rather, but it is long overdue."

With a vague feeling of unease, Emma settled into the chair and waited for her grandmother to continue. She could not remember when last the dowager had had such a solemn tone.

Grandmère held her gaze for a moment before she spoke. "You must understand that the last thing I wish to do is to cause you distress by bringing up painful events from the past. But I must so that I can share my concerns."

Her voice trailed away and with a sudden sense of intuition, Emma knew the subject her grandmother was so hesitant to broach.

Grandmère was right, she decided. This discussion was long overdue. And Emma intended to make it clear to her grandmother that she need not tread so carefully around the past.

"It's perfectly all right, Grandmère. You may talk to me of anything. I know the family has walked on eggshells regarding little Henry and Charles. Truly, though, it has been a very long time since the pain of losing my son has felled me. Do not fear that I shall crumble at the mention of his name. I have discovered I am made of stronger stuff than that."

Instantly, a sheen of tears glazed her grandmother's fine eyes. When she spoke, a bit of a rasp marred her voice. "What a gallant spirit you have, my dear. I know your marriage to Charles was not a happy one. I will not speak ill of the departed except to say that he was not equipped to deal with a woman of your intellect and temperament. I did know that you separated from Charles after you lost your baby, even though you put up a good front during holidays and family visits. You seemed much happier once you were out of Charles's house."

"Yes." Emma sighed, feeling this subject seemed like a long-faded bad dream. "After we separated, I found solace and purpose in Melham working to build the school and the other things I became involved with. There, I met any number of women who had lost children, husbands, friends, and siblings. Grief is a strange thing—one feels so lonely, low, and bereft. But I learned that suffering is the one thing we all have in common."

Silence held them for a few moments, until her grandmother cleared her throat. "This has been my experience too. And your words bring me to the reason I have touched these old wounds. Henry has been gone for almost eleven years and Charles almost six. You have finally returned to Society, where you belong. Yet I feel the pain of your past makes you fearful of reaching out to the possibilities the future holds for you."

Emma listened to the quiet, serious tone of her grandmother's voice and frowned a little in confusion. "I am afraid of nothing."

"Indeed? You have told me that you do not desire to marry again. I believe that is because of how badly you were hurt in the past."

Emma picked up the embroidered pillow from the chair next to her and held it close. "Forgive me, but I do not agree. Yes, I never again want to give a man the right to rule my life." Amelia's words about where there is love there is respect and protectiveness instantly came back to her mind, but she pushed them aside. "But even if that were not the case, no gentleman has captured my interest."

Grandmère's lips compressed into a thin line. "It is time to tell you that I have always known of your attempted elopement with Devruex. I know you never wanted me to learn that you considered such a shocking action, but there is little I do not know about my family. I do not know what occurred to end your relationship with him, but I was not against your marrying him then, and I would not be opposed to it now. My dear, do not let old fears ruin the chance of finally finding true happiness. Besides, I do not know how you can possibly resist his elegant rascality."

"Grandmère!" Emma said, shocked beyond words.

Chapter Seventeen

At nine o'clock the next evening, Jack entered the tobacco-scented sanctum of his club, looking to distract himself from the black mood that had been plaguing him for days.

While at Woodhouse, he had worked his horses, studied detailed breeding charts, and even mucked out stalls. He had believed that the vigorous activity would put into perspective this ridiculous resurgence of his youthful passion for Emmaline.

But upon returning to Town this morning, he found himself wondering if she had risen early again to ride in the park. He'd been on the verge of ordering his horse to be brought around, when it hit him that he was about to chase after her again.

With a sense of self-disgust, he had spent the rest of the day attending to business papers and correspondence that had accumulated while he'd been away.

Unable to stand his own company any longer, he'd come to his club this evening for a welcome distraction. He intended to broach a fine bottle of brandy, perhaps play a bit of cards and spend the rest of the evening with a few friends.

Passing through the foyer, he walked into the dark-paneled main room and scanned the deep chairs and sofas scattered throughout the space. Immediately three men on the other side of the room hailed him. The Earl of Edgebrooke, Sir John Mayhew, and Mr. Phillip Collard were seated around a table playing cards, dressed in formal clothes. With an acknowledging nod, he crossed the room.

"Good evening, Devruex. Why don't you join us for a few hands before we break up?" the earl offered, pushing a chair back from the table with his black-slippered foot.

After exchanging greetings with the other gentlemen, Jack sank into the well-upholstered cognac leather chair and eyed his friends' attire.

"Gentlemen, are you coming or going?" he asked as the unobtrusive waiter brought him his usual brandy.

"Going," the earl supplied as he shuffled the deck of cards. "I have a family obligation to attend the Litchfield crush. However, I don't intend to put in an early appearance."

"I'm going as well," said the fair-haired Mr. Collard.

"I'm tagging along with Edgebrooke," Sir John said and grinned. "I wouldn't miss it because it is rumored that Lady Fallbrook will grace us with her presence. I've been trying to gain her notice, with little success. Maybe my luck will change tonight."

Realizing he was gritting his teeth at the mention of Emmaline's name, Jack picked up the crystal tumbler and took a substantial swallow of the warm, mellow liquor.

Edgebrooke dealt the cards with quick, expert fingers and said, "She is perfection. There is a vague rumor going around that you are acquainted with the lady, Devruex."

Devruex picked up his cards and a negligent glance told him he held a queen and a ten, suited. "Lady Fallbrook and I have a number of friends in common."

"I have heard that she favors Monteford," Mr. Collard said, picking up his cards and wincing.

The memory of Emmaline kicking Monteford returned. He could not prevent a derisive laugh. "No, she does not."

Suddenly, the affable atmosphere changed and three pairs of eyes lifted to him with varying expressions of interest and speculation.

Lord Edgebrooke's rich chuckle broke into the silence and his hazel eyes sparkled with wicked amusement. "I have always said you were a deep one, Devruex. Shall we change the topic, gentlemen?"

"Certainly," Sir John said quickly. "Your Circes is causing quite the stir. Do you believe she will be in prime form by the Severly?"

"I do," Jack said, relieved to talk of anything other than Lady Fallbrook. "She is an amazing animal. Over the last few weeks it's almost as if she senses that something important is about to occur."

"The odds have certainly been shifting," Sir John said. "It would be an amazing coup if she could best Grafton's filly. I always wait until the last minute to decide where to place my blunt. I look for some sort of sign."

"Such as?" Devruex asked, always curious about gamblers' superstitions.

Sir John shrugged. "I never know until I see it. I bet a monkey on Minuet when she ran in the Oaks a few years ago because a butterfly lit on her ear for a moment. She won."

"Your method certainly beats cross-referencing racing records," Edgebrooke said, discarding a card.

"Saves time as well," Devruex added.

Conversation continued among the four in a desultory fashion as Devruex played several hands. At a quarter of an hour to eleven, the earl glanced up at the ormolu clock on the massive mahogany mantel and tossed his cards into the center of the highly polished table. Sir John and Mr. Collard looked patently relieved, for neither man had won a single hand.

"I believe I have lost enough for one night," Edgebrooke said dryly, "and duty calls me to Litchfield house. Too bad you are not dressed, Devruex. No doubt we could hoax a quiz or two at such a squeeze."

"No doubt," Jack replied with a smile, rising as well.

"But I believe I shall spend the evening here, where it is much less crowded."

The three men then departed and Jack moved to his usual chair by the fireless grate. He was taking his time with his second brandy and speculating on whether Emmaline would attend the ball. Inexplicably, his mood had not much improved since arriving at his club. He picked up this morning's paper from the table next to his chair when a familiar drawl drew his attention to the entryway.

Monteford, dressed in black evening clothes, walked in. The instant he saw Jack, he caught himself and hesitated.

Jack eyed him coldly, as Monteford approached and seated himself in the chair opposite him.

Anger warred with disgust within Jack and again he lamented the fact that Monteford had been too craven to accept his challenge. He continued to stare at Monteford as the nervous-looking man settled into the chair and crossed one leg over the other.

"Good evening, Devruex. I see you are not going to the Litchfields'. I thought I would have a drink or two before putting in an appearance," he said with a brittle little laugh, but Jack did not mistake the wary glint in his eyes.

The waiter approached with fresh glasses of brandy, and after Monteford accepted his, Jack waved the man off and sent Monteford a level look.

After taking a generous swallow, Monteford chuckled again. "Come now, Devruex, do not tell me that you are willing to let a woman—any woman—damage our years of friendship."

At the cavalier words Jack felt his body tense.

The look of amused hauteur left Monteford's fair features and he lowered his gaze to the glass in his hand.

Weaving his fingers together, Jack watched Monteford squirm for a moment longer. "I can think of nothing else important enough to cause such a thing to come to pass," Jack said bluntly. "Certainly not any petty misunderstanding over cards or horses could ruin a long-standing and valued comradeship. No. I judge that if two old friends are about to sever their friendship a lady certainly ought to be behind it."

As Jack spoke, Monteford's head slowly came up. Jack felt that at any other time he would have been amused at his gasping fishlike expression.

"Dash it, Dev, this is ridiculous. Lady Fallbrook is an attractive filly but I vow I was only up for a little fun—no harm done. She is certainly not worth this dustup." This time, his attempt at a dismissive chuckle failed miserably.

Pushing his chair back with such force that Monteford flinched, Devruex stood up, his black brows drawing together in a harsh line.

"Gad, Monteford, when did you turn into such an ass? If you ever insult the lady again be prepared to name your second. Is that clear enough?" he said in a calm voice.

"You know I'm not proficient with either swords or pistols," Monteford sputtered, staying seated.

"Then your choice is simple," he said and strode out of the room, leaving Monteford gaping after him with a look of alarm blanching his features.

As Devruex crossed the foyer, the major domo quickly approached. "Shall I call your carriage, your lordship?"

"No, I'll walk. Be so kind as to send my coach home," he instructed, accepting his hat and walking stick from the precise little man.

He left the building, and long strides took him through the lamplit streets of this fashionable part of London back to Leicester Square.

As soon as his butler opened the black lacquered front door, Devruex swept past him and crossed the foyer to the staircase. Taking the stairs two at a time, he saw his valet on the landing looking down at him with an expression of surprise on his round face.

"Bring me some evening clothes, Preston," Jack directed. "The double-breasted jacket with the claw-hammer tails will do."

"Right away, your lordship. You shall certainly make an entrance at this hour," he said with the familiarity of long service.

"The late hour won't matter. I am going to the Litchfield ball," he said, loosening his neckcloth as he continued to his bedchamber.

Chapter Eighteen

"Good Lord, it's warm in here," Emma said, putting the back of her hand to her cheek.

"Lud, yes," Amelia agreed. "Have you ever seen so many people crowded into one room? But it is one of *the* balls of the Season."

They stood on the edge of the dance floor, between two tall pedestals supporting massive urns filled with wilting flowers. The twelve-piece orchestra could hardly be heard above the din of six hundred people talking and laughing. Even so, the most important members of the Polite World filled Lord and Lady Litchfield's massive octagonal-shaped ballroom.

Emma had lost sight of her grandmother shortly after they had arrived an hour ago. Thank goodness she and Amelia had found each other or she would have been utterly bored swimming around in this packed pond.

Even so, her gaze swept the guests, looking for a certain pair of broad shoulders and black hair. She knew the time must be past midnight, and once again, there was no sign of Jack Devruex. Maybe she would not see him again for thirteen years, she thought with bitter humor. Because of the intense way their kiss had affected her, the idea of never seeing him again no longer gave her any comfort. She fanned herself, feeling restless and jumpy.

Just then, Amelia put her hand on Emma's arm. "Unless I am mistaken, it looks as if Lord Edgebrooke is coming directly toward us. This must certainly be attributed to you, Emma."

"Why me? I have never met the man," Emma said with a laugh, glancing over to see a tall handsome man with dark brown hair threading his way through the crowd toward them. "He is rather a Corinthian, isn't he?" she said, thinking him almost as handsome as Jack.

"Mmmm, rather. Oh, I do believe Sir John Mayhew is also heading in our direction. You should feel excessively flattered, my dear." This last bit was spoken behind her fan, for both men were almost upon them.

Composing her features to her most serene and confident expression, Emma smiled. She thought the gentlemen managed quite elegant bows, in spite of the crowd pressing so close.

After greeting them, Amelia, with a charming lack of subtlety said, "This is Lady Fallbrook, of course."

Emma smiled, bowed slightly to both men and said good evening.

"Lady Fallbrook, I can finally say the Season is a success," Lord Edgebrooke said as his friend chatted with Amelia.

"Oh? How can that be? The Season is not yet half over." Emma found the teasing twinkle in his hazel green eyes charming.

"Why, everyone knows the Season could only be considered successful if one has had the good fortune to make your acquaintance."

Emma laughed at his blatant flattery and decided that the earl had a way about him. Certainly, his brand of charm was not as potent as Jack's, but impressive nonetheless.

Suddenly, over his shoulder, she caught sight of a fair-haired man and her smile froze. Lord Monteford was looking at her with an expression that could only be described as beseeching.

She instantly thought of Mrs. Willoughby and wondered what the volatile woman was doing this evening. Odd, she had never before wondered what a mistress did in her spare time. There had been something in Mrs. Willoughby's aggressively proud demeanor that made Emma believe she would not like the way her protector was behaving at the moment.

Fervently, she hoped that Monteford would not be so impertinent as to address her. She had steadfastly ignored his notes begging her forgiveness, hoping he would just give up bothering her. Unfortunately, he was proving annoyingly persistent.

Although his unwanted advances had disconcerted her, it had been deliciously satisfying to kick him last week. After all, she had come to London looking for a bit of adventure, she thought, allowing her gaze to move coolly past him.

"Lady Fallbrook, shall we brave this mad crush and attempt to get near the floor?" the earl asked. "Earlier, I noticed a few brave souls dancing."

"Yes, why not be intrepid?" Emma said, amusement glinting in her dark blue eyes. Taking his arm, she glanced back to see Amelia still engaged with Sir John but she could no longer see Monteford among the mingling throngs.

As Lord Edgebrooke guided her through the crowd, Emma noticed Amelia and Sir John following close behind.

"I daresay that Lady Litchfield is excessively pleased with herself this evening," Lord Edgebrooke said conversationally.

"No doubt. I heard that no less than three ladies have already swooned," Emma replied as a group of dandies parted to let them through.

"Nothing is more likely to guarantee the proper cachet than a few fainting spells amongst the guests," the earl agreed with an air of mock gravity that matched her own.

Even though she was thoroughly enjoying Lord Edgebrook's company, after the disappointment of Lords Darley and Monteford she would not be so quick to consider the handsome earl as a potential paramour. But at least he was an attractive distraction from the intrusive thoughts of Jack.

To her surprise, there were indeed a few brave couples attempting to dance in the meager space to be had on the floor. She and Amelia did their best to converse with the two gentlemen, but it proved difficult over the general noise. They watched the dancing for some minutes before an odd shiver on the nape of her neck made Emma glance around.

Instantly, her gaze locked with a pair of eyes as black as night.

Frozen, she stared as Jack, his heart-wrenchingly handsome features hard with determination, weaved his way through the densely packed guests.

"I say, Emma dear, are you feeling well?" Amelia whispered at her side.

With tremendous difficulty, Emma pulled her gaze from Jack and turned to see the concerned curiosity in her friends' blue eyes.

"Of course. Why do you ask?" Even to her own ears her voice sounded a little tremulous and strained.

"Because you look a little flustered. Only a little, mind you. But I have never known anything to fluster you. Even the time the wheel broke on the coach we were in, you behaved as if the tea water was not hot enough."

Taking a deep tremulous breath, she smiled at Amelia's description.

"Pay no mind to me. In truth, I am unused to such crowds and noise. I am rather out of practice you know."

Amelia sent her a disbelieving look. "But I have been to any number of your parties at Maplewood and you are the most accomplished hostess of my acquaintance. You certainly have not been a hermit."

Emma forced a laugh at Amelia's observation, grateful for the distraction. Even so, she cast a furtive glance toward Devruex. He was still coming directly toward her. She recalled his strong hands pulling her against him and felt a shiver cascade down her body despite the warmth of the room.

"Can you honestly compare this evening to any normal mode of entertainment?" Emma stated, barely paying attention to her own words. "I have never entertained one-fifth this number in my home. I'm just out of practice at this kind of thing."

"Oh, tosh. You are—" Amelia stopped and put her hand on Emma's arm. "Oh look! No, don't! Devruex is making his way toward us. Blast this dreadful crush, it will take him twenty minutes to reach us."

At Amelia's words panic gripped her chest even tighter. Not yet! she thought, casting a slightly desperate look around for an escape. "Why don't we move to the other side of the room? It may be cooler," Emma said in an inane attempt to avoid Jack. It was too soon after their kiss! It would be impossible to face him at this moment with any composure.

"Don't you want Lord Devruex to come over?" Amelia asked in a low voice. "It was so gallant of him to come to your rescue at Vauxhall Gardens."

Galvanized by the fact that Jack was less than ten yards from her, she pasted a bright smile on her lips and turned to Lord Edgebrooke and Sir John.

"I beg you to excuse me, but I see my grandmother trying to gain my attention."

"It would be my pleasure to escort you to the dowager duchess," Lord Edgebrook offered in a tone of voice that would, at any other time, have been quite flattering.

"How kind," she said quickly, knowing she must seem the veriest oddity, "but that won't be necessary."

She turned on a heel, but not swiftly enough to miss the surprised expressions on their faces, and began to work her way through the crowd.

Panic aided her flight and she refused to look back in case Jack was right behind her. She realized that she was receiving some curious glances—after all, the sight of Lady Fallbrook crossing the room unescorted was unusual—but she did not care. Something in Jack's expression had set alarm bells off in her head.

A moment later, she came to a wide French door. She grasped the handle, turned it, and slipped out to a wide flagstone terrace. Quickly, she closed it behind her and inhaled deeply, feeling as if she had just escaped something she had no desire to face.

As she stepped farther onto the terrace, a cool breeze brought the scent of lilacs across her heated skin. The sudden quiet was a welcome balm to her fevered thoughts.

Guided by the golden light spilling from the windows, she took the wide stone steps down the terrace into the well-manicured garden below.

She walked until she came to a bubbling fountain ringed with lanterns and dropped her shawl on the stone bench next to it. Tilting her head back, she gazed up at the dark velvet sky. The vast expanse was almost as dark as Jack's eyes.

She should not have come tonight, she told herself fiercely. After her recent conversations with Amelia and Penelope, and then Grandmère—well, she was in no mood to be at a party.

Especially one attended by Jack Devruex.

A moment ago, when their had eyes met, the shiver of awareness that hit her in the pit of the stomach brought her grandmother's words back in full force—*you are fearful of the possibilities the future holds for you.*

At first Emma had dismissed the words out of hand, but now a niggling feeling told her she needed to consider if there were any truth to them.

She stood there, struggling with emotions she did not want to examine, when a husky, hauntingly familiar voice spoke behind her. "Emmaline, don't you think it's time we talked?"

Chapter Nineteen

Startled by Jack's sudden appearance, Emma whirled around to see him standing by a low hedgerow. What she could see of his expression in the low light emitted from the lanterns caused her heart to hammer.

She considered his question and everything within her shouted *NO*. To talk of the past would not only be pointless, but unbearably painful. Swallowing hard, she could not seem to find her voice.

Evidently, he was in the mood to be patient, for he stood still and let his words hang between them.

A breeze ruffled his black hair as her gaze roved over his features. Again she felt a stab of pain at all the lost years that had wrought so many changes in him.

Finally, unable to stand the silence stretching tightly between them, she said, "What could we possibly have to talk about after thirteen years, Jack?"

"Does the amount of time really matter, Emmaline?"

She met his gaze, and the bold look of demand and intimacy sent her insides quaking. Instinct told her this conversation was moving in a dangerous direction.

Walking a little closer to the fountain, she forced herself to gain control of her agitated emotions.

He took a step closer to her. "Considering the kiss we exchanged last week I find your behavior inexplicable."

At the challenging tone in his voice she gave a wry laugh. "My behavior is inexplicable to me, as well."

"You said you hated me. Why? You left me on that muddy road."

Again, she could not mistake the demand in his deep voice. Yet beneath the caution she saw in his near black eyes, she thought she saw a flash of desire and possessiveness and her breathing grew shallow in response.

But it was his words that she could hardly take in. Did he really blame her for not eloping with him? Could he really have no idea what his defection cost her? From the hard line of his jaw and compressed lips, evidently not. This realization shocked her to the core.

As their gazes held and clashed, she clenched her fingers into fists and fought to keep the tremor from her voice. "I did not leave you! I just went home. But you never came back!"

Her angry shout startled them both. But strangely, saying the words aloud after so long felt very good.

She watched his long fingers rake impatiently through his hair. "I never came back because you married Charles Fallbrook shortly after we parted." His voice now held a hint of anger as well.

"Because you never came back! I waited three months for you to come back. Every day I waited, expecting you to come up the drive, but you never did. You broke my heart."

In one stride he closed the space between them and swept her into his arms with fierce strength.

Balling her fists against his chest, she buried her face against his shoulder.

"Tell me, Emma. Tell me everything."

His husky whisper, spoken against her temple, seemed to knock down the last barrier, and the details of her painful past came tumbling out. "I felt so lost and foolish. I did not know what to do. I wrote you letters I did not send, because I was still so angry with you. But weeks went by and I realized that you could not have loved me."

She hated the way her voice broke, but felt powerless to stop the flow of words.

"I had known Charles all my life, and with my mother and my uncle pressuring me the whole time, I grew numb. After months went by, I quit waiting for you and told myself that I could forget you. Charles and I married and I was relieved because my family seemed happy at last. I did not start hating you until—" She tried to choke back the sentence, for it was too painful to finish.

His hand stroked the length of her back and she could feel the warmth of his body through her thin gown.

"When did you start hating me? I need to know, Emma."

Suddenly, she wanted him to know it all. Every sad, ugly truth of it. "Did you know I had a child?" she whispered.

"Yes." His words were more of a rumble in the ear she pressed against his chest. "I heard you had a little boy."

"Yes. Then you must also have heard that he died," she whispered, barely able to choke out the words.

"I did. I am so sorry, Emma."

"Henry was almost nine months old when he became ill with a terrible lung ailment. After—after a time hope was lost. During the funeral, my husband told me that he wished it had been me instead of our son who had died. I left him that day and started a new life in Melham. I began to hate you when I realized that if only you had not been drunk and lost the night we were to elope my life would undoubtedly have turned out in a vastly different way."

Her anguished voice trailed away but she did not move away from him. Neither spoke and the feel of muscular arms and his cheek against her temple calmed her quaking limbs.

She knew not how long they stayed this way, embracing in the warm night air. Slowly, though, being in his arms became an intolerable comfort. She felt too unsure of her emotions—and his—to be soothed this way. Opening her hands, she pressed them against his chest and an instant later she was free.

She found the look on his face unreadable as she said in a much more composed voice, "I had no intention of telling you any of this. In truth, I doubt these thoughts have been fully formed in my mind until this moment. But returning to London has brought so many memories back—it's as if I barely know myself anymore."

She paused, but he did not speak and continued to gaze at her with an intense yet unreadable expression.

"Truly, my life has been very fulfilling these last six years," she continued quickly. "Nevertheless, I am sure this has been something like letting poison from a wound, and there is no need to fear that you shall have to suffer through another outburst."

She made a heroic effort to inject a light note in the last sentence, for now that her emotions were spent, embarrassment began to set in at exposing so much of her feelings to him.

"Damn it, Emmaline, do not slip back behind that perfectly polished mask after what you just shared with me."

She could find nothing to say, feeling oddly empty after her outburst. Turning her head away, she looked out over the lantern lit garden.

"Marry me."

The firm, huskily spoken words had the effect of a pistol shot upon her overwrought senses. Whipping her head back to him, she stared for a moment, hardly believing she heard him correctly.

"Have you gone mad?" she whispered.

There was a tenderness to his laugh she had never heard before.

"You cannot deny what is between us. I now see what happened in a different light, Emma, and there is much we have to discuss. But for now—marry me."

Moving to the bench, she picked up her violet silk shawl. "Really, Lord Devruex," she began in a surprisingly composed voice, "there is no need to be so gallant."

Sweeping past him, she refused to meet his gaze and hurried up the path. She could sense him right behind her and as she ran up the wide terrace steps he caught up with her.

"Emma, don't—" His words were cut off by a sudden burst of raucous laughter from a nearby crowd of young people playing some sort of game with one of the ladies' fans.

She glanced back to see Jack's frown as he was forced to pause to let one of the dandies by. Emma took the opportunity to quickly cross the terrace and slip back into the house, where the sudden lights and noise dazzled her terribly confused senses.

Chapter Twenty

"You are here rather earlier than I expected. Was the Litchfield ball not to your liking?" Sally Willoughby asked coyly as she reposed upon the chaise in her salon.

Monteford had arrived a half an hour ago and had gone straight for the brandy. To her exasperation he had not said a word, not even complimenting the emerald green lace negligee she wore.

Sally watched him drink a quarter of the bottle—his expression growing more sour with each swallow—before she asked him the question.

Instead of answering her, he sloshed more brandy into his glass and slumped down in the chair with a grunt.

Sally pouted, yawned, and went back to flipping through a magazine. As much as his behavior annoyed her, she knew that he would not speak until he was good and ready.

He continued to drink and she continued to read until the candles burned low. Finally, Monteford turned blurry eyes to her and said, "I'm in the suds, Sal."

She laughed at his slurred voice. "Whatever are you talking of?"

"M'grandfather has cut me off."

The starkness of the statement and the desperate tone beneath the brandy-induced slur made her sit up and stare at him in alarm.

"Cut off!" she squealed. "What do you mean, *cut off*?"

Monteford pushed a pale lock off his forehead. "The old man says that I have to marry—now."

Sally thought a moment, then relaxed a little. "Well, he has been after you to get married for years." She hoped it was just the amount of liquor he had consumed that made him so dramatic.

"Yes, but this time he says he's stopping the blunt until I present him with my intended bride."

Sally tossed the magazine aside, jumped up from the chaise, and began to pace from one end of the room to the other.

"What about your mother? Surely she will see to your bills?" *And what about my bills?* she wondered in growing alarm.

Monteford shrugged and slid farther down the chair until his chin rested on his chest. "Perhaps, but not enough. There is nothing else for it—I'm going to have to find a wife."

Sally stopped her pacing to stare at him with narrowed eyes. "Is this why you have been making a cake of yourself over Lady Fallbrook?"

At her sharp tone his expression turned petulant. "I have not made a cake of myself over her. It's that blasted Jack Devruex."

His odd reference to Lord Devruex did not deter her. "Do you want to marry Lady Fallbrook?" she demanded.

"I don't believe she will have me," he mumbled.

"So you do want her!" she shouted as she threw her hands up. "No! I will not have this. Anyone but Lady Fallbrook. There must be someone else you can marry." This was terribly distressing. If Monteford married Lady Fallbrook it would be much too lowering. Everyone would know that he wanted the beautiful widow more than he wanted her. "You cannot want to marry her!"

"Of course I do. Who would not? Blast Jack Devruex. If he had not stepped in, I would have had a chance with her."

She put her hand on her hip. "Why are you angry with

Devruex? It is not his fault if she favors him. Besides, your grandfather will come around. How can he not?"

"Because that is how he is," he said, sloshing some of the brandy onto his shirtfront. "I must find a wife as soon as possible—and she must have a decent dowry."

Sally shook her head in dismay. "This is an odd and insulting subject to be discussing with me."

"Who else would I talk to about this?" he said, looking up at her with an expression in his eyes that convinced her that this was serious business indeed.

Gooseflesh rose on her arms as she gazed around the room. Everything she had worked so hard to get was in jeopardy. She said nothing and he continued.

"My marriage, or lack of one at this point, affects you as much as it does me. I honestly do not know how long I can afford you, Sally." He finished with a bitter laugh and took another swallow of brandy.

Sheer panic softened her scorn as she sat down next to him. "Surely, if you spoke to your grandfather again—"

"Hah," he interrupted, "you do not know the old man. It's not just that he wants me to marry—he has made it expressly clear that he is disappointed in me. He wishes I were more like Devruex," he said through gritted teeth. "My God, if only I had Devruex's money I'd tell the old man what he can do with his ultimatums. I must find a wife, but in the meantime, I must find a way to raise some capital before my situation becomes embarrassing."

Sally frowned as they sat in silence for some time, Monteford gazing morosely into his brandy glass. Suddenly, something of great import occurred to her. Reaching over, she grasped his left hand in both of hers and looked beseechingly into his eyes.

"So, Monty dear, does this mean I cannot have a new ensemble for Ascot?"

Chapter Twenty-one

Emma awoke very late the next morning. Her head throbbed, but she forced herself to sit up when Milton quietly entered the room and opened the drapery. The maid said she would bring her mistress chocolate and fruit, and then quietly left the room.

Sitting up in the canopied bed, Emma gazed out to the garden, which looked so colorful and inviting in the late-morning sun.

Instead of enjoying the view, she was trying—with difficulty—to absorb last night's events.

She cringed remembering the way she allowed the bitter, accusing words to spill out.

With a quick movement, she kicked aside the covers and padded over to the window.

And yet . . . somehow she felt different. To her amazement, the lump of nagging sadness and resentment that had sat in her heart like a stone for more than a decade had disappeared.

She checked again. Taking a deep breath, she closed her eyes and felt a definite lightness that had not been there before.

"What an odd creature I am," she whispered aloud.

But Jack Devruex was even odder, she thought as she watched a robin bathe in the fountain near a weathered iron sundial.

The way he had held her while she poured out her pain

and anger had made her feel strangely safe and comforted. Even now her cheeks grew hot as she remembered the gentle way he had stroked her back as she told him how much she hated him.

It was the most intimate experience of her life, she admitted to herself as the robin fluffed, shook his wings, and flew away.

What must he think of her? she wondered in growing embarrassment.

Actually, she knew the very painful answer to that question. He pitied her. She had sounded like some pathetic woman who had been pining over him for all these years, when he had obviously gone on with his life without giving her a thought until she came to London again. Baring her soul last night had made him feel pity and guilt. Why else would he have made such a hasty offer of marriage?

No doubt he was thanking his lucky stars that she had not accepted him. Now, he could dismiss any belated sense of responsibility over abandoning her all those years ago, she thought, pressing her fingers to her closed lids to stop the flow of tears.

Suddenly, the words he had spoken after their kiss at Vauxhall Gardens came back to haunt her—*you may hate me, but you want me just as much.*

Well, she was honest enough to admit that she no longer hated him, but what was she going to do with these even more disturbing feelings?

Just then, the door opened and Milton entered carrying a rosewood tray. "Your ladyship is in for a surprise," she said, placing the tray on the table between the chairs by the fireplace.

"Don't tell me there are more flowers from Lord Monteford," she said dryly. His floral arrangements and beseeching notes had arrived every morning since his insulting behavior at Vauxhall Gardens.

"No. Lady Tunbridge is downstairs wanting to speak with you."

Emma looked at her maid in surprise, then glanced at the clock on the mantel. It said half past ten. "Heavens, what is Penelope doing here? She usually isn't out of bed for hours."

"Shall I send her away?"

"Of course not. Bring her up and she can share my repast," she instructed as she moved to the foot of the bed to retrieve her wrap, grateful to have a reprieve from her own company.

"Very good, my lady, I shall have another cup sent up."

"Thank you." Tossing the blush pink garment over her arm, Emma crossed the room to the door that led to the water closet.

By the time she had completed her ablutions and smoothed her hair, Penelope had entered the bedchamber.

"Well, this is a turn," Penelope said with a wry smile.

"Indeed. I cannot recall when you have ever been up and out this early," Emma said with a gentle laugh. "Will you join me? We have chocolate and lovely oranges and pears."

"Oh, yes, please. I left the house without any breakfast," Penelope said, removing her peach confection of a bonnet and tossing it on the bed.

Once both ladies were seated and holding delicate porcelain cups filled with fragrant warm chocolate, Emma took a good look at her friend.

Despite the warm color of her apricot spencer, she looked pale and there were shadows under her green eyes.

"As happy as I am to have you share my breakfast, I know you came for a reason. Tell me what is wrong."

Penelope sighed deeply. "When I awoke this morning there was a jewel box next to my pillow."

Emma sent Penelope a look of understanding, for she knew this subject had long been a sore spot for her friend.

"What was it this time?" she asked, picking up an orange wedge.

"A whacking big emerald brooch," Penelope replied glumly. "And again, no note. I just wanted to throw the thing across the room. I found it so patronizing I could not stand it another moment—so here I am."

"I'm sorry, Pen. I know how much this upsets you. Have you ever considered telling Tunbridge that you would prefer that he not give you any more jewels?"

"I just cannot. It would sound so silly."

Emma thought for a moment before replying. "At least explain to him how you feel."

"What on earth could I possibly say?" she asked, setting her cup down. "After more than ten years of marriage, I cannot very well tell him that I would prefer it if he did not give me such extravagant gifts if he does not love me."

"Why not? I think that is a perfectly reasonable thing to say, especially since that is exactly how you feel."

Penelope bit her lip and remained silent for a moment or two. "I don't know. It feels like such a ridiculous thing to complain about. How many women would love to be in my place? I do not wish him to think me churlish."

Emma reached for the chocolate pot and refilled Penelope's cup. "He is your husband, Pen. I believe if you explain your feelings to him, you just might be surprised. Have you ever considered the idea that the jewels are his way of expressing his love for you?"

Penelope shook her head sadly. "I used to wonder if that were the case. I have always loved him, even though our families arranged our marriage. There have been times when I hoped that he might have a higher regard for me than mere affection, but my hopes have always been dashed. He has never once told me he loves me."

"That does not necessarily mean that he does not," Emma said in an attempt to comfort her friend.

"How hard is it to say the words?" Penelope asked with a bemused shake of her head. "Surely, if he loved me, when our children were born he would have told me. But, no, a sapphire diadem appeared next to my pillow when Freddie arrived and a diamond demi-parure after Jane."

Emma considered her words for a moment. She had al-

ways liked and admired David Tunbridge and felt his
steady, confident nature was a good balance to Penelope's
more sensitive personality. Truly, anyone observing the earl
and his countess together would be convinced that they
were besotted with each other. Emma wanted to offer her
friend support, but she did not want to sound at all critical
of Tunbridge.

"But he does not give you jewelry only after important
occasions," she gently pointed out.

"No, sometimes jewels show up for no reason," Penelope said with a shrug. "I just do not know if I have the
nerve to approach him about this."

"Good heavens, Pen, it is not at all like you to be so
timid. Take the risk. The reward may be well worth it."

Penelope stared at her with vulnerable green eyes. "Perhaps you have the right of it. I shall just have to be brave
and tell him my thoughts and feelings. I am so glad you are
here, Emma. Writing all this in a letter would have been impossible."

Emma smiled gently. "Yes, this is much more convenient."

Penelope picked up her cup again and gave a gusty sigh.
"I am tired of myself. Let us speak of more pleasant things.
I am so pleased that you will be staying at Longdown for
the races."

Emma's brows rose in surprise. "You are under a misap-
prehension. I have not even received an invitation from the
Duke and Duchess of Severly."

Penelope's knowing grin immediately raised Emma's
suspicions. "But your grandmother did. She told me last
night at the ball that she accepted for the both of you."

"Well! I wonder when she was going to see fit to tell
me," Emma said archly. "This is most vexing. I really have
no desire to attend."

Frowning curiously, Penelope asked, "Why? Because
Devruex will be there?"

"Frankly, yes," Emma replied as she brought the cup to her lips.

"But why? I thought his gallantry over Monteford's insults had smoothed over the past."

Emma contemplated the dregs of the chocolate lingering in the bottom of her cup before answering. "Not exactly. Jack asked me to marry him last night."

Penelope's cup rattled in its saucer. "What? Are you joking?"

Emma spread her hands wide. "Would I joke about this?"

"I suppose not. I am just so shocked. How could you let me rattle on the way I did? Apparently, you have been withholding a great deal from me."

"Yes," Emma sighed, "I have."

"Well, I am going to sit here until I know all the details," Penelope said, settling more comfortably into her chair with an expectant look on her face.

Emma hesitated, but the determined set of Penelope's jaw convinced her that she meant her words. With a sense of unburdening herself, Emma relayed the main points of her recent encounters with Jack as her friend listened with rapt attention.

"Wait a moment," Penelope said when Emma had finished speaking. "Are you saying that you believe that Devruex asked you to marry him out of some belated sense of guilt and honor?"

Emma pulled her dressing gown closer, wrapped her arms around her waist, and looked away from Penelope's serious gaze. "Why else? I have not so much as caught a glimpse of him in the last thirteen years. Why else would he offer marriage in such a precipitous manner?"

Penelope gave a wry laugh. "The one thing that I have learned after more than a decade of marriage is that I have little understanding of how the male mind works. Perhaps Devruex has never completely fallen out of love with you?"

"Hogwash! Love does not work that way," Emma said, feeling sad and vehement all at once.

"Who is to say how love works? I certainly do not know. I do know that Devruex has never married in spite of being chased by any number of desirable ladies over the years. I do know that he has never kept a mistress for more than a Season or two and that they have all been blondes or red-heads."

Emma looked at Penelope in complete bafflement. "What does the hair color of his mistresses have to do with the price of spices in India?"

"Because," Penelope replied impatiently, "none of them have had your coloring. It's as if he could never bear to spend time with women who resembled you. That has to mean something."

Emma could not help smiling at her friend's rather strange logic. "I do not care if it does mean something. You are very mistaken if you think I would consider that he meant his proposal."

"Can you honestly tell me that since coming to London none of your old feelings for him have returned? I have seen for myself the way you look when he is around."

After the intensity of her encounter with Jack last night, she could no longer pretend that she was indifferent to him. "That may be so. I cannot deny that he is an exceedingly at-tractive man. But I would be ten times a fool to risk my heart with him again."

Penelope affixed her with a perceptive green gaze. "I am going to use your own very wise words, my dear. 'Take the risk. The reward may be well worth it.'"

Chapter Twenty-two

On Thursday afternoon, Jack rapped on the dowager Duchess of Kelbourne's door and waited impatiently for her exquisitely correct butler to answer. This was the third time this week that Jack had called and he wondered if it would also be the third time that he would be told that the dowager duchess and Lady Fallbrook were not at home.

Not only had he visited three days out of the last four—he had also taken early-morning rides in Green Park every day since the Litchfield ball, but he had yet to encounter Emma. To his growing frustration, she seemed to have disappeared from London, which only made everyone gossip about her even more.

As he tapped his silver-tipped walking stick against his gleaming black Hessians he decided that if he was turned away again, he was going to have to come up with another plan to speak to Emma. He did not know exactly what his next move would be, but he intended to speak to her.

Finally, the heavy door swung open and Jack was amused to see that the butler did not look at all surprised to see him.

"Good afternoon, Simms. Need I ask if the duchess and Lady Fallbrook are receiving visitors today?"

Simms performed a very correct bow, and when he straightened, Jack did not mistake the hint of a smile at the corner of his mouth.

"Her grace and Lady Fallbrook are in the drawing room, my lord."

Simms stepped aside, obviously expecting Jack to enter, but Jack was so surprised that he paused outside for a moment before stepping onto the black-and-white marble floor in the grandly appointed foyer.

The butler took his stick and black beaver topper and handed them to a young footman, then led Jack up the stairs and down a wide hall. Jack fought his impatience at Simms's measured pace.

Finally, Simms came to a door and opened it wide. Jack strode in as the butler announced him. He scanned the room and his gaze immediately lit upon the dowager duchess's white head and then—to his surprise—the Earl of Pellerton, who was seated next to her on the blue upholstered sofa.

Turning, he saw Emmaline seated across from them, dressed in a pale violet-blue gown that made jewels of her eyes. His pulse quickened.

Her posture was rigid and her beautiful features were utterly serene, he noticed with some annoyance.

The only thing hinting that all was not well with the elegant Lady Fallbrook was the unusual pallor of her cheeks.

For an instant, his gaze held hers, but he could not gauge any emotion in their cool depths.

"Lord Devruex!" The duchess cried in delight as she held out a fragile, beringed hand for him to salute. "How good of you to visit. I am sure you know Lord Pellerton," she said with a wave in the earl's direction.

"Of course, your grace," Jack replied as the elderly peer rose from the sofa. "How do you do, sir?"

"I have not seen you in a dog's age, Devruex," the earl said jovially after they had bowed.

Jack had always admired the handsome, engaging earl, even envying Monteford for having a grandfather he could be proud of.

From his open, friendly manner, Jack had to assume that

the earl was unaware that he had challenged his only grandson to a duel. With an inward shrug, Jack decided that suited him just fine.

Finally, fighting to keep his expression from revealing too much to the duchess and Lord Pellerton, he turned to Emma.

"Good afternoon, Lady Fallbrook. I trust you are in good health," he said, bowing deeply before her.

"I am perfectly well, Lord Devruex, thank you," she said in a polite voice. She even managed a smile that did not reach her eyes, he observed as he seated himself in the chair next to hers.

Now what? he wondered impatiently as the dowager duchess and the earl beamed smiles upon him.

It had been his hope that he would find Emma and her grandmother alone so that he could suggest that Emma take a drive in the park with him. But the earl's presence changed his plans. It would be rude to attempt to steal away one of the ladies the earl had come to visit.

"I am rather surprised to see you, for I had heard that you were off readying your wonderful horse for the Duke of Severly's race," the dowager said as she prepared his tea and handed him the cup. He was impressed that she remembered the way he liked it.

"I have recently spent time at my house in the country, but returned several days ago," he replied.

"I attended a race a while back and saw your filly nose out Grafton's," the earl said. "Terribly exciting. Do you think she can do it again?"

Jack shrugged. "Circes certainly has the heart for it, but racing is a tricky thing. All the horses entered into the Severly are exceptional animals. Any horse in the field can win."

His gaze strayed to Emma and he wondered if she remembered all the conversations they had had years ago about starting a racing stud. She had not only been supportive, but had made suggestions that showed she was truly interested. As a young lady she had been an impressive horsewoman, and when he had watched her ride away the morning they spoke in Green Park, it was obvious that her skills had only improved.

Emma kept her serene gaze fixed upon her grandmother.

"Well, my granddaughter and I are certainly looking forward to watching your horse run. We shall be attending the races and the ball afterward." The duchess shot a pointed look at Emma.

Jack watched with great interest as this comment finally elicited a reaction from Emma. She compressed her lips slightly and set her cup and saucer on the table next to her.

"I had not intended to go to the Severly races. In fact, because of correspondence I recently received, I shall need to return home shortly."

Jack felt his grip tighten on the delicate cup as her words sank in.

A flash of unthinking anger had him about to speak, when the dowager duchess said in a clear, crisp voice, "Nonsense, my dear. I am quite counting on you to attend with me. Surely, whatever calls you back to Yorkshire can be postponed for a week or two?"

"Indeed," the earl said in a cheerful, yet firm voice, "the Severly is all the crack—it really cannot be missed. I shall be attending with my grandson. I do not put too fine a point on it to say that we would both be desolate if you were not there."

Jack saw her swallow at the mention of Monteford and for a brief instant her gaze met his. The moment of shared amusement before her polite mask slipped back into place had his pulse quickening.

The duchess picked up a biscuit from the tiered tray on the table before her and placed it on her saucer. "We have already accepted the invitation. Really, it would be too disappointing for you to leave Town right now."

Emma's shoulders lifted briefly. "I doubt that the duke and duchess would be disappointed by one less guest."

"You are mistaken," Jack said. "There are a number of people who would be greatly disappointed if you did not go to the Severly races."

She turned her soft blue gaze to his and he tried his best to read them. Did he see vulnerability, mistrust, determination? Yes, he believed he did.

But what he did not see, as he continued to gaze into her beautiful eyes, was the anger that had been there the night they had danced together at the Colhurst ball.

He felt his chest tighten at this new knowledge and had to fight the desire to reach out and touch her porcelain-smooth cheek.

A moment later, the sweep of her lowered lashes hid her eyes from him and she sighed softly.

"Nevertheless," she said, turning to her grandmother, "I shall be leaving London this week."

Struggling to hold his tongue, Jack glanced at the duchess. Despite her polite half smile, her gaze had a look of such steely determination he suddenly knew where Emma got her stubborn streak.

"Well, we shall certainly discuss this later," she said with a sniff. "More tea, Lord Devruex?"

Before Jack could reply, the door opened and Simms stepped in and bowed. "Lady Cowper and Lady Westlake, your grace," he announced precisely.

As the elegant ladies swept into the room, Jack and the earl stood up. Glancing at the grand clock standing next to the door, Jack realized that he had already stayed for nearly half an hour.

Knowing what a stickler the dowager duchess was for protocol, Jack regretfully decided to take his leave, lest the duchess take him in dislike for overstaying his welcome.

Evidently, the earl had the same thought, for once the greetings had been exchanged with the newcomers and they had been seated, the earl remained standing as well.

"As much as I hate to leave this delightful company, I

must be off," the earl stated as he bent to salute the duchess's hand.

"And I must follow Lord Pellerton," Jack said, looking directly at Emma, who seemed to be finding her cup extremely fascinating.

"How very good of you both to depart," Lady Cowper said with a saucy grin, the egret feathers in her bonnet dancing merrily. "It will be much easier to gossip about you if you are not here."

Everyone laughed at this quip and the duchess said, "I do hope you both will visit again soon."

Jack did not think that it was his imagination that her gaze lingered upon him fondly. Well, at least he could count on the formidable old lady's support, Jack thought with grim satisfaction.

He had definitely botched it the other night by the fountain, he admitted. His bald proposal had obviously been too abrupt after Emma had revealed such painful emotions to him.

Nevertheless, despite his uncharacteristically maladroit behavior, he had no intention of letting her run off and leave him again without letting him explain his own feelings.

With another bow and a last glance to Emma, whose expression was again politely unreadable, Jack followed Lord Pellerton from the room.

Once downstairs, both men stood in the foyer for a moment as attentive footmen produced their hats and walking sticks.

"Walk with me a bit, Devruex," the earl said after instructing Simms to have his tiger follow him in his curricle.

With a feeling of curiosity, Jack said, "Certainly, sir," as they walked down the marble steps to the sidewalk.

They strolled a little ways down the tree-lined, sun-dappled street before the earl finally spoke.

"I hope I don't need to tell you that I hold you in high esteem and have enjoyed watching your growing success over the years," he said without preamble.

Although Jack and the earl had always been on the most cordial terms, Jack now noticed a slight coolness in the older man's slightly raspy voice. "I am most gratified, my lord," Jack said as a mail coach lumbered by.

"Forgive my blunt speech, but you may not be aware that my grandson and Lady Fallbrook are developing a very promising understanding. I know that you would not wish for your interest in the lovely lady to cause any awkwardness."

Jack stopped and gazed at the proud-looking old man with a slight frown. After silently cursing Monteford for his spineless conduct, Jack said, "Lord Pellerton, your kindness to me over the years has meant a great deal to me. I mean no disrespect when I inform you that your opinion of Lady Fallbrook and your grandson is erroneous. And forgive my bluntness, but even if it were not, I have no intention of being gentlemanly and bowing out."

The earl's stunned expression gave Jack no satisfaction as they stared at each other in silence for several moments.

Suddenly, the earl's face broke into a crinkled smile. He then began to laugh heartily as he leaned upon his ornately carved walking stick. "Good for you, young man. But I must tell you that I have known the formidable Duchess of Kelbourne for close to forty years. And after spending a little time with the enigmatic Lady Fallbrook I can see that the apple has not fallen far from tree. I'd be willing to bet a monkey that she won't have either of you."

Chapter Twenty-three

Emma had never pushed her horse, Titus, so hard. But as they flew across the deserted expanse of Green Park, she sensed that the gelding was reveling in the exertion as much as she.

As the horse's hooves pounded the ground and the wind whipped her sheer veil, Emma attempted to gain control of her chaotic emotions.

"I am right to leave," she aloud. "I would be a fool to stay."

As she bent low over the pommel and guided the horse in a wide arc, her heart clenched at the scene she had just left at the townhouse. She was still reeling from the first argument she and her grandmother had ever engaged in.

Ever since Jack had called a few days ago—throwing her into a state of tension and confusion—Grandmère had been pressuring her to attend the Severly races.

Emma had steadfastly resisted her grandmother's reasoning, cajoling, and arguing until she felt her nerves were stretched beyond their endurance.

Though it was difficult to disappoint Grandmère, she would leave London and not continue to put herself in harm's way—meaning anywhere near Jack Devruex.

After all, it had taken every ounce of her self-control to be in Jack's presence and ignore the smoldering, challenging look in his eyes as he sat next to her.

What did he want? she wondered as she urged Titus to

run faster. Out of hand, she discounted Jack's hasty offer of marriage. Yet she could not forget the deep timbre in his voice as he told her that she wanted him.

With a fluttery little catch in her heart she told herself it was pointless to keep lying to herself about this.

She did want him. Everything about him made her senses vibrate. His dark eyes, angled cheekbones, and square jaw had always been, to her, the masculine ideal of beauty. His broad shoulders, tapered waist, and muscular legs caused butterflies in her stomach.

Yes, she wanted him.

But every logical instinct within her shouted that she would be risking tenfold the pain she had experienced thirteen years ago if she indulged her desire.

She had come to London with the vague, half-formed plan to find romance, but never once had it been her intention to gamble her heart again.

Thirteen years had not been enough to rid herself of these intense, consuming feelings for him, she thought angrily.

She must go home before she did something foolish.

Unfortunately, Grandmère had been equally determined that she should stay.

This morning, as Emma had been helping Milton finish packing, Grandmère had appeared at her bedroom door, dressed for the day in a gray-blue traveling costume.

Emma had been surprised to see her up so early, but the militant gleam in her eyes had made Emma stop folding a paisley shawl.

"Milton, you will prepare a case with the appropriate clothing for a two nights' stay at the Duke and Duchess of Severly's estate. There will be a horserace this afternoon and a ball this evening. I shall expect my granddaughter to be the most fashionable lady there."

Emma had shifted her surprised gaze to the stout maid and was greatly exasperated to see a look of satisfaction on her features.

"At once, your grace." Milton had curtsied quickly and then begun pulling gowns from the trunk.

Emma tossed the shawl aside. "Grandmère, I would ask you not to order my maid to do something expressly against my wishes. Milton, continue packing."

Milton hesitated, looked mutinous for a moment, then sent the duchess a defeated look and resumed her task.

Her grandmother had puffed herself up and tried to stare Emma into acquiescence. However, Emma was more than determined to hold her ground as Milton darted nervous looks at each of them as she continued to fill the trunks.

After a moment or two of staring at one another across the bedchamber, Grandmère tried a different strategy. "This ridiculous situation has my nerves quite agitated, Emmaline. Why are you being so wretchedly difficult?"

"I am certainly not trying to be difficult, Grandmère. I am merely preparing to return home."

"Stuff and nonsense. I insist that you accompany me to Longdown. I have already accepted the invitation for both of us."

"That certainly does not signify. And I have absolutely no desire to go to Longdown."

"You are being childish," Grandmère had accused.

"And you are being a martinet," Emma had snapped back, unable to control her exasperation.

They went back and forth in this manner for some time, each becoming more frustrated with the other, before Emma had had quite enough.

"I have no intention of continuing this pointless argument, Grandmère. I shall go for a gallop to give us both a chance to cool off. But I intend to leave for Melhem before midday." With that, she had actually walked out on her stunned grandmother, something she had never done before.

Now, as she continued to ride at a fast clip, she felt heartsick at exchanging such harsh words with her beloved grandmother.

Even so, she still had no intention of going to Long-down.

Feeling her temper cooling, she reined Titus slightly, but still let him run. Although she felt a certain amount of relief that she would soon be returning to the familiar routine of her life in Yorkshire, there was a heavy weight in her heart that forced tears to her eyes—but they were not completely caused by her argument with Grandmère.

"I got over him before. I'll get over him again," she said aloud, and Titus twitched his ears in response to the torment in her voice.

Just then, she caught sight of a shiny red gig being pulled by two white ponies a short distance away.

"Not again," she said through gritted teeth as the driver vigorously waved in her direction.

Reflexively, she slowed Titus to a trot and watched in dismay as Mrs. Willoughby waved even more vigorously, practically falling out of the little conveyance in her efforts to gain Emma's attention.

With a gusty sigh, Emma turned Titus toward the gig. Lord knew if she did not, Mrs. Willoughby would likely chase her down.

"Good morning, Mrs. Willoughby. We really must stop meeting this way," she said as she rode up next to the beautiful courtesan.

Mrs. Willoughby gazed up at her from beneath a bonnet trimmed in gathers of pink ribbon. Even from her perch on the horse, Emma could see that there were dark circles under her finely tilted eyes.

"I was hoping that I would find you riding this morning. In fact, I have come early for the last three mornings looking for you. It's been most inconvenient."

Emma suppressed a laugh. Despite Mrs. Willoughby's ill-mannered behavior, Emma was surprised to find that she could not take her into complete dislike. Perhaps it was because there was something rather artless about her outrageousness, Emma mused.

"Forgive me for not being clairvoyant," Emma said, but there was no sting in her tone.

"Oh, never mind," Mrs. Willoughby said, alighting from the gig. "Are you going to get off that beast so that I can speak to you, or must I crane my neck?"

Emma instantly recanted her charitable thoughts. "I don't believe I will stay after all. Good day."

Mrs. Willoughby put up a staying hand. "I'm sorry. Don't be annoyed. You are annoyed, are you not? It is hard to tell because you always sound so dashed polite."

Emma hesitated. After her row with Grandmère she was in no humor to listen to Mrs. Willoughby accuse her of trying to steal Lord Monteford from her again.

"Please stay, your ladyship. There is something important I must speak to you about."

Emma gazed down at the younger woman and saw the look of urgent pleading in her gaze. Shrugging, she said, "All right then, but I have only a few moments."

She meant it, for she wanted to return to the townhouse and smooth everything over with Grandmère—as long as the iron-willed old lady did not continue to pressure her about going to the races.

After dismounting from Titus, they walked to the little clump of trees where they had talked before. Emma waited impatiently as Mrs. Willoughby paced upon the grass, her soft pink gown and pelisse giving her an innocent appearance.

"I might as well just say it. Monteford and I have parted ways."

At this blunt statement, Emma raised a brow and said, "I do not know why you would think that I care." Actually, she did wonder what became of mistresses under such circumstances. She could not imagine that Mrs. Willoughby had enough money to support herself in the manner she so obviously was accustomed to.

Mrs. Willoughby bit her lip. "That is not really the reason I hailed you. You see, his grandfather is being wretchedly tightfisted and has cut Monteford off without a farthing until he finds a wife with plump pockets."

"So?" Emma was beginning to lose what little patience she had.

"You mustn't judge him too harshly because he has grown rather desperate in the last few days. You see, he cannot pay his bootmaker and—"

"Mrs. Willoughby, would you please get to the reason you insisted upon speaking to me?"

"All right, all right. I have always had a certain regard for Devruex and would hate to see him hurt—"

"What does Devruex have to do with this?" Emma blurted in sudden alarm.

Mrs. Willoughby put a hand on her hip. "If you will stop interrupting me, I will tell you. Yesterday, Monteford had one of his men take a packet of money to the jockey who will be riding Devruex's horse in the Severly race that is taking place today."

Emma frowned. "A packet of money? Whatever for?

"You are rather green, aren't you?" Mrs. Willoughby said with a snort. "To bribe him, that's why. Monteford is desperate for blunt and is betting that the horse will lose. He wants to make sure that is exactly what happens."

Emma felt not only shocked, but bewildered. "Bribe the jockey? But you must be mistaken. Monteford is a cad, but I cannot imagine that he would be so dishonorable."

"I told you, he is quite distraught. He's rather spoiled, you know. Besides, he's grown to hate Devruex of late. Devruex left Town yesterday, so I could not tell him about the packet. I thought you would be going to the races and could warn Devruex. Maybe there will be enough time to switch jockeys."

Emma's thoughts were spinning with the possible ramifications of what she just heard. "Good heavens, I can hardly countenance what you are saying."

Spurred by this devastating news, she grabbed her trailing

hem and whirled toward Titus, when a sudden thought had her tossing a question to Mrs. Willoughby. "Why tell me?"

She knew without question that Mrs. Willoughby held her in great dislike, so this gesture was quite inexplicable.

The younger woman lifted her shoulders in a brief shrug. "When we spoke before, I said that you could not know what it was like to struggle. You told me that I knew nothing of your life." She turned her gaze away, and suddenly looked almost shy. "Well, something about the way you said it made me think that you were not such a toffee nose after all."

Their gazes met for an instant. The completely unexpected feeling of understanding that passed between them had Emma smiling warmly as she reached for her horse's bridle.

It took a couple of tries, but Emma soon managed to get herself back on Titus. Swinging the horse around, she looked down at Mrs. Willoughby. "Thank you for telling me this. May I ask what you intend to do now that you and Lord Monteford are no longer, er, keeping company?"

A beautiful smile came to Mrs. Willoughby's perfectly formed lips. "Not to worry, my lady. The Earl of Edgebrooke and I are already in negotiations. So far, I am most impressed with his generosity. And he has promised to teach me how to drive a proper carriage."

Shaking her head wryly at Mrs. Willoughby's resilience, Emma could not resist asking a question that had crossed her mind once or twice before.

"May I be so impertinent as to ask what Mr. Willoughby thinks about . . . all this?"

Mrs. Willoughby sent her a cheeky grin. "Gracious me! There is no Mr. Willoughby. I gave myself a husband because it sounds more respectable."

Chapter Twenty-four

"We must reach Longdown before the race starts at two o'clock," Emma stated as a groom helped her into the open barouche.

The coachman, a big man who wore his livery with obvious pride, jumped up to the seat and took the ribbons. "Not to worry, m'lady. This team is the best we got. All four are well rested and ready to run," he said as the groom scrambled up next to him.

The slight frown creasing her brow cleared a little at this reassurance. Settling next to her grandmother against the soft leather squabs, she said, "Thank you, Richards," just as the carriage took off with a jerk.

As they rolled down the quiet lane beneath the midday sun, Grandmère sent her an encouraging smile. "We have a good two hours and these meets never start on time."

"I am depending on it," Emma said as they turned onto a busier thoroughfare.

However, her anxiety grew as they came upon a bottle-neck of carriages turning onto Park Lane.

"I should not have taken the time to change clothes," she said as she craned her neck to get a better look at the confusion in front of them. A liveried postilion, his white wig askew, was struggling to gain control over a team of six horses while nearby coachmen and grooms shouted abuse upon him.

"Don't be silly. A habit is a most inconvenient garment

anywhere but atop a horse. Besides, you must look your best today."

Emma shifted her gaze to her grandmother, who looked fresh and lovely in an ensemble of jonquil yellow and cream silk. Her bonnet was quite the most beribboned thing Emma had seen since coming to London.

"What I wear is of little interest to me," Emma said, glancing down at the fitted lavender bombazine pelisse she wore over an ice blue gown.

When Emma had returned to the townhouse after her encounter with the intriguing Mrs. Willoughby, Milton had been surprisingly quick with producing the fashionable garments—for Emma had previously directed that a simpler traveling costume be readied for the trip to Yorkshire. Evidently, her grandmother had not given up and continued to collude with the maid to convince Emma to go to Longdown.

Setting aside her concern over Jack, Emma smiled as she recalled Grandmère's reaction at being told Emma now wanted to go to the races.

Grandmère's expression had changed from firm-jawed and militant to shocked and speechless as Emma ran up the stairs, tossing the most important details over her shoulder.

Now, as her grandmother chatted happily next to her—enormously pleased that she had won her way—the carriage circumnavigated the tangle of coaches and entered the turnpike heading south. Soon, they left the noise and congestion of London for green hills and pastures that seemed to stretch to the horizon. Richards, handling the ribbons with expert ease, gave the horses their heads.

Although the sun shone brightly, a few fat, bubbling clouds in the distance caused Emma a fleeting moment of worry. Her brows knit in a slight frown as she watched the clouds above the passing trees.

It would be too horrible not to reach the Duke and Duchess of Severly's estate in time to warn Jack about Monteford's scandalously dishonorable action. With her heart racing as the horses' hooves clopped along the road, she gripped the side of the carriage tightly to prevent herself from shouting to Richards to hurry.

She thought about the importance of this day to Jack, for the Jack Devruex she had known so long ago could only have dreamed about owning a horse good enough to have a chance at winning such an important race.

She had known, even at the green age of eighteen, that his desire to build a successful stud was wrapped up in the shame he felt at his father's infamous squandering of the family fortune.

And somehow, she thought with a poignant sense of pride, despite all the obstacles he had undoubtedly faced, he had managed to become a nonpareil in the rarified atmosphere of horseracing. What better way to restore his honor than to triumph at the sport of kings?

Leaning forward slightly, she willed the horses to run faster. As the driver expertly tooled the team around a slower, closed coach, she relaxed slightly and sat back again.

She could not allow his dream—everything he had obviously worked so hard to achieve—to be destroyed in this nefarious way.

Suddenly, she wished she had not protested when Jack had challenged Monteford to a duel.

"Don't worry, my dear. Richards is a true knight of the ribbons. We shall be there in no time."

Emma sent a tremulous smile to her grandmother and relaxed her grip. "I am sure we will. It is just that it would be so dreadfully unfair if Jack lost because his rider was bribed."

Scowling, Grandmère shook her head. "Tell me in detail what that wretched woman told you."

As Emma recounted the particulars of her conversation with Mrs. Willoughby, Grandmère clucked and murmured.

"And you believe her?" she asked when Emma had finished.

"Oh, yes. In her demeanor, her expression, there was every evidence of honesty. Even if I did not believe her, I could not set aside the possibility that her tale was true. I would never forgive myself if Jack lost when I could have warned him."

The carriage swayed as Grandmère reached over and placed her hand on Emma's. "I am so happy, Emma."

Instantly, at the dewy look in the old lady's eyes warning bells went off in Emma's head. "Grandmère, I do not want to even hazard a guess as to what you are thinking. The only reason I am going to Longdown is to warn Lord Devruex."

With a snort, Grandmère sent her a knowing look. "Lord Devruex? A moment ago it was Jack."

Feeling anxiety at her uncharacteristic lapse of propriety, Emma opened her mouth to protest, but Grandmère's raised hand halted her words.

"I shall not say another word. We shall be there within the hour and you can tell Devruex about Monteford's shocking ploy and then we can all enjoy this lovely afternoon."

Suddenly, as if in defiance of her grandmother's declaration, a cloud moved in front of the sun and dimmed the brightness of the day. Glancing up, Emma watched in dismay as the clouds—only an hour ago so white and fluffy in the distance—hung low and dark in a clump almost directly above their heads.

"Oh, no," Emma said in dismay.

Richards and the young groom next to him also noticed the threatening sky. "Your grace, looks as if we might be in for a spring shower. Should I pull over and fold up the top, or take a chance that we can outrun it?"

"We cannot stop!" Emma said before Grandmère could answer. A low rumble of thunder had her grandmother looking at her askance.

"But, my dear, the weather looks quite threatening. Let

us stop for ten minutes. We will get soaked if we do not fold up the top. I am sure the shower will pass quickly."

Turning her anxious gaze to the terrain ahead, Emma bit her lip. There were no clouds in the distance. "It most likely is not raining at Longdown. I am so afraid we will be too late," she said as a big, cold drop of rain hit her forearm. "Richards, do you have the time?"

Shifting the reins to one heavily gloved hand, the coachman produced a timepiece from one of his pockets. "Ten minutes after one of the clock, m'lady."

A few more drops fell on her. "How far away are we?"

Richards took a moment to adjust the reins before answering. "Maybe another thirteen to fifteen miles, m'lady."

Emma squeezed her eyes shut as the sporadic drops turned into a definite sprinkle. This was disastrous, she thought as she impatiently removed her bonnet and tossed it across the carriage to the seat opposite her.

"Emmaline, we must stop. We shall get drenched if this continues." Grandmère's tone was beginning to sound a bit cross.

"I cannot express how vitally important it is that we reach Longdown before the race starts," Emma said, wiping raindrops from her cheek. "We cannot possibly risk being too late."

The rain started in earnest and Richards had to slow the team's tempo as the road grew slick. The young groom, who had kept his gaze on the road ahead and his mouth closed since the carriage had left the townhouse, sent her a quick, concerned glance over his shoulder.

Grandmère made an aggravated noise deep in her throat. "Of course I understand. But this is folly, my dear. I know we are still some distance away, but I keep telling you that the race will not start right on time. Now, Richards, pull this rig over."

"No!" Emma cried, turning away from her grandmother to speak to the driver's wide back. "Richards, a gentleman I know has a horse entered into the Severly Stakes. I have information that his jockey has been bribed to lose the race. Even though it's raining, do you think we have enough time to make it by two o'clock?"

Richards said nothing and slowed the barouche—but he did not stop. The young groom's shoulders obviously tensed as he stared up at the driver, rivulets of rain running down his check.

Emma held her breath and waited, relieved that Grandmère did not immediately order him to stop again, despite the increasing force of the rain.

"Well, m'lady, we won't be able to run them on this wet road, but I'll do my best to get you there right soon," Richards said over his shoulder in a calm voice.

At this, Emma turned beseeching eyes to her grandmother, whose beribboned bonnet was beginning to droop in what threatened to become a downpour.

"Oh, bother," Grandmère said with a gusty sigh. "Neither one of us will be at all presentable. Drive on, Richards."

Leaning over, Emma pressed a damp cheek against her grandmother's and pulled her into a tight embrace. "Thank you," Emma whispered as she pulled back.

"Oh, bother," she said again, but there was a soft warmth in her tone this time. "You are right. I would feel utterly wretched if Devruex was not warned. Do not worry. We will brave this horrid weather and arrive on time."

As the rain soaked them, Emma smiled warmly, relieved that they were still moving. "We must."

"Are you still going to tell me that the only reason this undertaking is so important is because you wish to be a Good Samaritan?"

Emma lowered her gaze from her grandmother's perceptive blue eyes. The last thing she wished to do was examine the myriad emotions coursing through her right now. It seemed as if she had been on a pendulum since coming to London. But she refused to think of anything except getting to Longdown before the race started.

Shrugging, she did not answer her grandmother and

tilted her head back to look up the sky and let the spring rain hit her face.

Neither spoke for several minutes as Emma turned to watch the countryside, which reminded her of a lovely watercolor painting, passing by.

"I shall not press you further. But I will share something with you that I want you to think about."

At the unexpectedly gentle tone in Grandmère's voice, Emma looked over curiously and waited for her to continue.

"Before the Colhurst ball you asked me why I had not married again after your grandfather passed away. I recall that I made some offhand response."

"Yes, I remember," Emma said, wondering what the old lady was getting at.

"I should have told you what I really felt," she said, smoothing the damp skirt of her yellow gown. "I did not marry again because I never met a gentleman who ever came close to making me feel the way your grandfather did."

Emma watched her grandmother's usually proud expression soften at the onslaught of distant memories. Knowing how difficult it was for her grandmother to show any vulnerability, Emma said, "Thank you for telling me this," and felt grateful for the rain masking her unexpected tears.

Chapter Twenty-five

Ten minutes later the downpour stopped as suddenly as it started and the sun shone with dazzling brightness upon the wet countryside—and also upon the wet occupants of the barouche.

But Emma did not care, for once they turned onto the road leading to the village of Westerham, Richards was able to put the horses back into a fast rhythm and she began to feel that they were making up some lost time.

Grandmère recovered from her moment of poignant emotion and soon was complaining about the sad state of her clothing. "This is terrible! I have no idea how far behind our baggage coach is. Who knows how long it will be before we will have dry clothes."

Emma smiled a little at her grandmother's grumbling but did not reply. There were a few more carriages traveling along the road and she hoped they would not slow their progress.

"We'll be there shortly, m'lady," Richards said with a practiced flick of the reigns.

At his confident tone, Emma felt her shoulders relax a bit. Suppressing a pang of guilt over practically forcing them to drive through the sudden shower, she glanced up at the bright blue sky. Thank goodness the day was warm, she thought as they entered the village square.

The narrow cobbled streets were crowded with coaches

and baggage carts and servants in every style and color of livery.

As they went by a posting inn, Emma noticed the stable yard was full of carriages with stable boys scrambling to unharness tired horses.

"I am sure this village has not seen this much activity all year," Emma commented as Richards carefully navigated through the serpentine lanes.

"Indeed," Grandmère replied. "Evidently anyone not fortunate enough to be a guest at Longdown is crowding into the meager lodgings offered here."

Emma felt another wave of relief when they left the village and entered a narrow road canopied by trees, which led to the Severly estate. When she finally saw the open, ornate iron gates, she was practically bouncing up and down with impatience to reach Jack.

Immediately upon passing through the gates, Emma allowed her anxious gaze to sweep across a beautifully proportioned Tudor mansion situated in the middle of a wide expanse of flat green parkland.

Off in the distance to the left, there were hundreds of people—some on horseback and in carriages—dotting the lawn.

From the pattern of the banners fluttering in the breeze, she could see the racecourse was set up in a large oval.

They continued up the curving graveled drive until they caught up with a short line of carriages depositing their occupants beneath the wide marble portico.

Unable to contain herself a moment longer, Emma stood up before the carriage came to a complete stop.

"Emmaline, what on earth—"

"I must find him," she said quickly, sending an apologetic smile to her alarmed grandmother. Before the groom could act, she had opened the carriage door and jumped down without the aid of the steps.

"Emma! You cannot go traipsing around the estate looking like a drowned cat," Grandmère called after her.

Unheeding of anything but her desire to find Jack, Emma hurried down the drive. She stumbled a little as her damp skirts hampered her stride. But she soon recovered and continued around the large house toward the back, where she assumed the mews were located.

Once she rounded the side of the house, she was suddenly confronted by a hive of activity. Men and boys dressed in the latest fashions to the most serviceable clothes rushed around the stable yard in a seeming chaotic dance.

She darted around a gray steed, whose rider wore silks of blue and gold. The groom holding the horse's bridle shouted, "Hey there, miss, you should'na be back here. The races will be startin' in a few minutes."

Emma whirled around, her gaze darting from one man to the next as the horses cantered passed her. A fashionably dressed man trotting next to a beautiful chestnut thoroughbred came toward her.

"Please, sir," she said loudly, hoping she could be heard above the din. "Have you seen Lord Devruex?"

The gentleman hesitated, his surprised gaze sweeping over her bedraggled appearance. "He's at the other end," he said with a jerk of his head in that direction. "The fillies are racing next." And with that, he went trotting off again.

Pushing a lose tendril off her cheek, she wended her way through the crowded yard, past the mews, in the direction the gentleman had indicated. Despite feeling utterly relieved that she had arrived before the race started, she still felt panicked that she might not be able to locate him amongst the hundreds of men bustling around the stable yard and mews.

Just then, as she paused to let another horse and rider by, she saw him some twenty feet before her. Her breath caught in her throat as she moved toward him.

He was speaking to two other men, his tall, athletic frame magnificent in a dark blue jacket, tan leather breeches, and gleaming Hessians. His head was bare and his black hair swept away from his strong features. He was quite the handsomest thing she had ever seen.

At that moment he turned. She met his riveting dark eyes and stopped.

She watched as a flash of surprise crossed his features and his gaze swept her from head to toe and back up again. Without a word to the men he had been addressing, he moved toward her with long strides.

"My God, Emma, are you all right?"

"I had to tell you," she paused and took a deep breath. "Mrs. Willoughby informed me this morning that Monteford has attempted to bribe your jockey. I am sure she told me the truth, Jack."

She looked up at him, keeping her voice low so that only he could hear her. Darting a quick glance around her, she could not mistake the avid attention she was receiving from the other men.

Jack said nothing and his gaze continued to rove over her features. There was an expression in his eyes she had never seen before.

"There is still time," she said quickly. "Is there another rider—"

"You came here to tell me this?" he cut in, a smile lurking at the corner of his mouth.

"Of course I did," she said impatiently, alarmed at his nonchalant attitude. "Your jockey has been bribed."

"I know."

Emma stared at him in surprise. "Y-you know?" she stuttered.

"Yes, Tommy came to me right after he received the packet from Monteford."

Emma blinked several times, at a complete loss for words. Suddenly she felt utterly deflated and a bit foolish. Glancing down at her damp, wrinkled clothing she felt painfully self-conscious. "You trust your jockey?" she asked a little lamely.

"Implicitly. I told him to keep the money, for even if

Circes loses it won't be because Tommy did not try his best. But he refused, saying that it would be bad luck to do so."

"Oh," she replied, unable to think of anything else to say.

Suddenly, it occurred to her with mortifying clarity that she could have chosen any number of less embarrassing ways to handle this situation. For one, she could have simply sent a note with a groom on a fast horse.

But no, she had to be so dramatically foolish as to come herself, she thought with a feeling of shame and self-recrimination.

"Emma, you came all this way and got soaked in the rain just to inform me that my jockey had been bribed?"

With a sigh, she nodded her head. After all, he wouldn't believe her even if she did deny it. "Yes, it's rather silly, isn't it?" But something about the glint in his eyes made her heart start to pound rapidly.

"Very," he agreed with a tender smile.

In the next moment, he pulled her into his arms and his warm lips were suddenly on hers. Startled almost out of her wits, she put her arms around his neck to keep from losing her balance.

At first, the feel of his body overwhelmed her overwrought senses and she could hardly form a coherent thought. But a moment later, the strength of his arms encircling her body and the tenderness of his lips washed away the vestiges of shame, doubt, and fear. She began to kiss him back with all her heart.

As the kiss went on, she became vaguely aware of whistles and laughter swirling around them. Reluctantly they both pulled back and Emma felt as if she could willingly drown in the tender passion she saw in his eyes.

"Looks like you've been right compromised, Devruex!" someone shouted good-naturedly. The men nearest them laughed and a few more good-natured teases were made as Emma's cheeks began to flame. For his part, Jack looked unfazed and kept his gaze on hers.

"Beggin' your pardon, my lord," said a spry-looking

man standing some dozen feet away, holding a cap between his hands. "Circes is balking at having the saddle put on her back."

Jack sent the man a brief nod before turning his intense gaze back to her. "Emma," he said, his hands warm through the sleeves of her pelisse, "I have so much to do in the next few moments—"

At the concern and hesitation in his tone she sent him a tremulous smile and said, "Good luck. I'll be watching the race."

Keenly aware of the amount of male attention she was receiving, she lifted her chin, turned, and walked back through the crowded stable yard with the same elegant pace she would use crossing a ballroom.

With an indescribable feeling in her heart, Emma started off toward the racecourse.

The jumble of emotions crowding her thoughts had her feeling almost dazed and she put her shaking fingers to her lips.

It seemed rather amazing to her that something as basic as a kiss could throw her past, present, and future into such confusion. But it really wasn't just the kiss, she mused. It was Jack himself. Still touching her throbbing lips, she decided that now was not the time to try to sort out her chaotic emotions.

Looking down, she winced at the state of her clothes. Not only were they horridly creased and still damp, but her excursion to the mews had added a border of dirt several inches wide to the hem.

As she continued toward the crowd, she spared a moment's lamentation that there was no time to change her clothes—even if Milton had arrived with the baggage coach.

She drew nearer and it became instantly clear that no one seemed to mind that the racing had not started yet. People milled about in groups, some by carriages with picnic baskets and some beneath open-sided tents.

As her gaze scanned the numbers of ladies—garbed in all the hues of the rainbow—it became painfully clear that no one else had been caught in the rain.

"Emma!"

At her name she turned to her left and saw Amelia rushing toward her, wearing an apple green ensemble and holding aloft a pink parasol. Roger was close behind his stunned-looking wife.

"Good afternoon, Amelia. Good afternoon, Roger," Emma said as they rushed across the perfectly manicured lawn. "Surprised to see me?"

"Lud, yes!" Amelia said as she stopped, her gaze moving up and down Emma's clothes. "Last we spoke you were on your way back to Yorkshire. What are you doing here looking like you fell in a trough?"

Emma laughed and spread her hands wide. "I changed my mind about coming this morning. Grandmère and I got caught in a sudden shower on the way here. I don't want to chance missing the race by taking the time to change."

Amelia still stared, her expression a picture of consternation, but her husband stepped forward and offered his arm.

"I think you look charming," he said with a broad smile. "They will be parading the fillies any moment, so let us find a good vantage point."

Emma smiled at Roger, deeply touched by his gallant behavior. As she took his other arm, Amelia recovered her composure and said, "Yes, we must find a good spot so we can cheer for Circes."

With the dashing Roger Spence-Jones between them and the subject of Emma's clothing being studiously ignored, the ladies chatted as they joined the rest of the highest-flying members of the beau monde.

As she and the Spence-Joneses made their way across the lawn toward the finish line, Emma became aware of how everyone was eyeing her curiously. With a philosophical shrug, she decided that she couldn't blame them and was grateful that she had never been a slave to fashion.

Dismissing the attention she was receiving, she became aware of her mounting excitement over the impending race. Even though she felt reassured that the attempted bribery had failed, the jockey's honesty did not necessarily ensure that Circes would win.

Suddenly, she was quite startled to see Monteford standing with a group of fashionables a few yards in front of her. He looked handsome and proud—and completely innocent of being capable of such a corrupt action.

A searing anger narrowed her gaze as she said to her friends, "I wish to speak to Lord Monteford. Do you mind?"

"Of course not," Roger replied affably, changing directions slightly.

"Emma," Amelia leaned forward and whispered, "do you think this is wise? He is standing there with . . ." Her voice trailed away as they drew near the group of people.

Monteford and the others turned at her approach. Emma was so riveted by his surprised and cautious expression that it took her a moment to notice the Earl of Edgebrooke on his left and—to her wide-eyed shock—the Prince Regent standing on his right.

Hesitating, she tightened her grip on Roger's arm as she fought the strong urge to flee. Stealing another glance at her clothing, she saw with a sinking feeling that the bright afternoon sun highlighted the dusty water stains on her pelisse.

Wincing inwardly, she thought it was one thing not to have a care about her appearance when she confronted Monteford, but quite another to look like a tatterdemalion in front of the future king of England.

In a haze, she heard Roger present her to Prinny, as her grandmother called him. She knew she must have curtsied, for on the way up she admired his parrot green waistcoat and somewhat florid, yet handsome, face. She noticed that he had put on quite a bit of weight since the last time they had met during her husband's funeral.

"My dear Lady Fallbrook," he cried in obvious pleasure, his rather prominent blue eyes taking in her clothing, "it is beyond a delight to see you after so many years."

"Thank you, your royal highness. Please forgive my strange appearance. I was caught in a sudden shower a little while ago." She was pleased that her tone sounded more casual than distressed. Even so, she spared a sympathetic thought for Milton and Grandmère. They had worked so hard, despite her indifference, to ensure she was the most modish lady in the beau monde and Emma had soundly ruined the illusion in one afternoon.

"Could this possibly be the *perfectly perfect* Lady Fallbrook?"

This question came from the very pretty lady standing next to Prinny, who had just been introduced as Lady Jersey. She giggled at her own quip and a moment later the other ladies in the group joined in, staring askance at Emma's clothes.

Before she could respond, the Earl of Edgebrooke stepped forward and drawled, "Indeed it is Lady Fallbrook. And she can even make a bit of mud look perfectly perfect."

Tilting her head to the side, Emma sent the earl a smile for his gallantry. She recalled how flattering she had found his attentions at the Litchfield ball and she also remembered Mrs. Willoughby telling her that morning that she was "in negotiations" with the handsome earl.

"Quite so, quite so," the Regent agreed with a hearty laugh, wagging his finger at her. "The tattle is that you are up to every rig and I can see for myself that you are. Your artless lack of vanity is quite refreshing, my dear Lady Fallbrook. I predict that a muddy hem will soon be all the crack."

Everyone but Lady Jersey laughed at this quip and Emma took the opportunity to look at Monteford. He met her gaze for a moment, before looking away.

She turned back to the Regent. "You are much too kind, your royal highness, and much too amusing."

Prinny preened a little and said, "Not at all, Lady Fallbrook. Now I insist that you and Mr. and Mrs. Spence-Jones watch the race with us. We have staked out a perfect view of the finish line."

At this unexpected honor, Emma and Amelia curtsied and Roger bowed. A cheer went up in the crowd and Emma turned to see that a dozen or so horses, their riders garbed in colorful silks, were being led to the opposite side of the oval course. With growing excitement she realized the first race was about to start. Lord Edgebrooke moved to stand next to her on the soft grass as the rest of the group resumed their conversations.

"I am much more interested in the next race. What say you, Lady Fallbrook?"

Hoping no one else caught the quick scathing glance she sent Monteford, she replied, "I am of the same mind, Lord Edgebrooke. My hopes are quite set on Lord Devruex's horse winning."

Despite her polite mien, Emma was experiencing a great deal of frustration. The presence of the Prince Regent prevented her from venting her disgust and anger at Monteford for his despicable attempted bribery. Even though she was furious, she would never consider creating a scene in front of Prinny.

Edgebrooke nodded slowly. "'Tis a very good field, but it is my personal opinion that the real race is between Devruex's Circes and Grafton's Prunella. My blunt is on Circes."

Emma decided that she liked Lord Edgebrooke even more and smiled up at him. She was taken aback to see that instead of returning her smile, he was eyeing Monteford coldly.

"So, Monteford," he continued, "I am sure you have placed a bit of the ready on your good friend Devruex's filly."

By his frosty tone, Emma suddenly suspected that Mrs. Willoughby had told her potential new protector of Monteford's shocking behavior.

In fact, after giving it a moment's thought, she could not imagine that someone of Mrs. Willoughby's temperament could keep such information to herself. Shifting her gaze to the fairer man, she gritted her teeth at his insufferably smug expression. The desire to expose him to the world as the dishonorable cad she knew him to be nearly overwhelmed her.

As he pulled a snuffbox from his breast pocket, Monteford said, "As much as I admire Devruex's training methods, I confess that I think Prunella looks to be the stronger horse."

Emma stiffened her shoulders and clenched her hands behind her back, for she itched to slap the knowing little smile from his lips.

"Is that so?" she said sharply. "I have a hundred guineas that says Circes wins. Would you care to meet that wager, sir?"

At her challenging words, she heard a murmur go through the group around her and caught Amelia—who was standing nearby—frowning slightly with concern and confusion.

"What, ho! This is delicious," the Regent said with a broad grin as he moved to stand closer to her. "I do believe Lady Fallbrook is an Original."

A look of alarm briefly crossed Monteford's face before he gave a forced chuckle. "Upon my rep, Lady Fallbrook, I would never be so ungentlemanly as to take a lady's money."

Fuming, Emma was about to call him a coward when Edgebrooke said in the same cool tone he had used before, "Then I shall make the wager on Lady Fallbrook's behalf." He then held out his hand to Monteford to seal the wager.

Monteford hesitated but Edgebrooke kept his outstretched hand before him. Everyone, including Prinny, watched with avid interest.

Emma saw the brief struggle in Monteford's eyes. No doubt he was wondering how he would cover such a sum if he should lose, Emma surmised cynically. An instant later the look of overweening confidence returned to his face and he shook Edgebrooke's.

"I will apologize in advance for relieving you of your blunt, Edgebrooke. One never knows how Fate will smile upon these events, but I would not be at all surprised if Grafton's filly takes the day."

Fate, my foot. Not bothering to hide her angry expression, Emma glared at him openly. How dared he, for his own selfish reason's, try to damage the man she loved? Emma thought in growing fury.

The man she loved.

The words reverberated through her mind, catching her by complete surprise.

The man she loved.

Her fury at Monteford—which only a moment ago seemed nearly uncontrollable—instantly vanished as the truth of the words began to sink in.

Strangely, she felt no surprise at the intensity of her emotions. What shook her to her soul was the realization of their true meaning. Since returning to London, her unanticipated feelings toward Jack were neither a sudden, irresistible desire, nor the leftover dregs of a youthful infatuation.

No, what she felt for him was a passionate love, deep and true. Taking a shaky breath, she felt the impact of this truth settle in her heart. She loved Jack Devruex. She had always loved Jack Devruex.

"Zounds!"

Lord Edgebrooke's oath pulled her from her thoughts and feeling a bit dazed she turned to him curiously.

"We were so engrossed in our conversation we missed

the first race. The fillies are up now," he said, pointing to the parade of horses being led to the start line.

With the air seemingly trapped in her lungs, Emma scanned the riders, looking for Jack's distinctive racing colors of cobalt blue and silver.

When she found them, she sent up a fervent prayer that Circes would have the race of her life. Emma's heart pounded as she watched the grooms helping the jockeys get the horses settled at the line. She wouldn't be able bear it if everything Jack had strived to achieve was dashed under this cloud of controversy.

She watched with anxious eyes as the jockeys struggled to hold the horses. The impressively tall Duke of Severly stood by, ready to drop a white flag to start the race.

An instant later, she jumped as a shout went up and the horses surged forward in a blur of long legs and flying manes.

Lifting a hand to shield her eyes from the sun, she hurried to the wood railing that encircled the course. The others followed and she found herself standing between the Earl of Edgebrooke and the Regent as the horses rounded the first corner.

Standing on tiptoe, she strained to distinguish one horse from the other. "Where is—I cannot see Circes."

"She is in the middle," Edgebrooke indicated helpfully as the horses, still in a tight pack, took the next curve.

Spotting the cobalt and silver amongst the riot of color she held her breath as Circes and three or four other horses began to pull away from the rest of the field.

"Capital! Capital!" Prinny said, clapping his hands as the other ladies waved their handkerchiefs with excited vigor.

Rounding the next curve, the horses surged into the straight with the jockeys bent low over their necks. The pack thundered past her and she closed her eyes, unable to look in case Circes was falling behind.

"Two more laps," Edgebrooke shouted over the excited cheering of the crowd.

Opening her eyes, she leaned forward to watch the horses take the inside curve. Her heart lurched to her throat when she saw a flash of crimson satin pulling ahead.

Cheers rose anew at this change in the leader, and her heart sank as Circes stayed in the middle.

"Crimson is the Duke of Kingston's color. His horse usually gets out early, but fades in the last quarter," Edgebrooke said, keeping his narrowed gaze on the field.

This information did little to calm Emma's pounding heart as she watched the horses, starting to spread out now, on the opposite side of the course.

She began to breathe again when the jockey maneuvered Circes into third place. *Run, run, Circes!* she silently shouted, gripping the railing with both hands.

"Kingston's filly is sure to lose her stamina soon," Prinny shouted. "It will come down to Prunella and Circes at the end. Both are in perfect position right now."

Kingston's horse still led, but Grafton's Prunella, her jockey wearing sky blue, was gaining as they turned into the next curve.

Just then, a tall, hatless man standing on the other side of the course distracted Emma's attention from the tense competition.

It was Jack and he was not watching the horses. She kept her gaze on him as he scanned the crowd. An instant later she was sure he saw her and she pushed away from the rail. Unheeding of anything but the need to reach him, she left her friends and began to hurry through the crowd.

Halfway around the course, heart pounding and breathless, she slowed her steps when she saw Jack striding toward her, his expression determined. He continued striding across the grass toward her, ignoring everyone else. She stopped and took a deep breath; there was so much she wanted to say, needed to say, to him.

She could not read his expression, but the intensity of his

dark gaze had her struggling to find her voice. Her desire had been to be near him as the race finished; it never occurred to her that he would not be completely focused on the tightly contested battle taking place on the turf.

He was less than three yards from her when a deafening cheer rose from the crowd.

Instantly, a dozen or more men surrounded him, and their hurrahs had him looking around with an expression of stunned surprise. Emma stepped back as they began to pull him toward the finish line, still cheering loudly.

She watched with growing delight as Jack resisted his friends' entreaties for a moment, then shrugged and sent her a wry grin.

With a joyous smile coming to her lips, Emma felt something within her heart—something that had been in bud thirteen years ago—now unfold into full bloom as the crowd swept Jack away to the winner's circle.

Chapter Twenty-six

Sitting at the dressing table in the charming bedchamber she had been appointed, Emma tapped her foot impatiently as Milton put the finishing touches on her hair. It was the most intricate and flattering hairstyle she had worn all Season, Emma decided as she looked at her reflection in the mirror. She had agreed to let Milton take the time to arrange her hair only to offset the dismal impression she had made earlier. But now she was growing increasingly impatient to go down to the ball.

"Gracious me! What's this? I cannot believe you are not ready."

Emma turned to see her grandmother standing in the doorway, looking glorious in a blue-gray evening gown that did wonderful things for her bright eyes and white hair.

"Milton is almost finished with me," Emma said with a smile as Grandmère strode in and sat down on a nearby chair.

"'Tis a miracle, your grace. Her ladyship has stayed still long enough to let me give her a proper hairstyle," Milton said, placing another pin in one of the coils on the back of Emma's head.

"Excellent, Milton. I still shudder to think of all the gossip floating around the house at this moment. Everyone is wondering what Lady Fallbrook will wear to the ball after her shocking appearance at the races today. So it is imperative that she look her best this evening. The gown is a perfect choice."

Emma had to agree. Earlier, after she had had a bath and sat in front of the fire drying her hair, she had decided to wear the most sophisticated gown she owned to the ball this evening. Made of deep purple, gleaming, tissue-weight silk, it gave her fine complexion an alabaster glow.

Fussing with her reticule, Grandmère sniffed and said, "I cannot believe I missed the race and all the excitement that followed."

"You did not have to miss the race. We certainly arrived in time," Emma replied, adjusting her diamond eardrops.

"Hah! As if I would allow myself to be seen by all the rank and fashion looking like a muddy urchin. No, I had to seek my room and hear later how Circes nosed out Prunella at the very last moment. Everyone says it was the most exciting race they have seen in years, and I missed it."

Emma smiled at Grandmère's grumbling as Milton finally professed herself satisfied with her mistress's appearance.

Jumping up, Emma grabbed her reticule and shawl from the bed and walked to the door. "Thank you, Milton. I am ready, Grandmère." With a trembling hand, she reached for the door handle, and a wave of nervousness gripped her heart.

"Are you well, my dear?" Grandmère asked softly as they stepped into the well-appointed hallway.

Emma gave a vulnerable little laugh. "Honestly, I am not sure. But I do know that if I do not leave this lovely room right now, I may lose my nerve."

She met her grandmother's startled gaze, relieved when Grandmère made no reply as they continued down the hall toward the staircase.

Muffled in the distance, Emma could hear the full orchestra playing a reel and her heart sped its beat in time to the lively tempo. She would be seeing Jack in a matter of moments.

Just then, Grandmère said in a conversational tone, "You may be pleased to know that Monteford left immediately after the race. The tattle is that he seemed to be quite upset and in a hurry."

This interesting bit of information distracted Emma from her growing anxiousness. "Did he? That is excellent. I will not have to kick him again."

Grandmère laughed at this and they joined several other guests at the staircase.

"By the by," Grandmère said as they descended, "have you been introduced to our host and hostess yet?"

Emma nodded. "You forget that I knew Severly years ago. But I did meet the duchess when I came in to change my gown. What a delightful creature! Such ease of manners and grace."

"I am sure the duchess was much too polite to gawk at your muddy hem," Grandmère said with a hint of asperity.

Emma only grinned as they left the dim hall and stepped into the dazzling light and festive noise of the ballroom.

Making a concerted effort to keep her composure, Emma immediately began to scan the hundreds of guests enjoying themselves in the large, mahogany-paneled room.

As her gaze was drawn to every dark-haired man in the room, she refused to think beyond the next moment. All she knew was that she desperately wanted—needed—to see Jack. She had no idea what she would say when she did. And she was keenly aware that an inexplicable fear still lingered beneath her desire to be with him.

"How does one bridge thirteen years in an instant?" she whispered, reverting to her old habit of speaking her thoughts aloud.

Feeling a gentle grip on her arm, she looked down and met her grandmother's perceptive, smiling eyes. "Why, with love, of course," she said softly, before turning to greet some friends.

At her grandmother's completely unexpected comment, Emma stayed very still for a moment and allowed the wisdom of the words to sink into her heart. Then Emma began to move through the crowd on her own, addressing people here and there, oblivious to the stares and murmurs she left in her wake.

Pausing by a column near an alcove to scan the room again, she overheard a lady on the other side of the column say, "Look, Edith, there is Baron Devruex! Oh, isn't he devilishly handsome? Those dark eyes give me the trembles."

With an amused smile, Emma renewed her efforts to locate Jack as the unseen Edith replied to her friend, "He is terribly dashing. I am so glad his horse won the race. The Duke of Severly is going to present the cup right before we go into supper. Perhaps at that time I can attempt to gain his attention."

Just then, Emma finally spied Jack standing beneath a large pastoral painting on the far side of the room. Her heart caught at how handsome he looked in his formal black evening clothes.

The atmosphere was definitely congratulatory, as any number of ladies and gentlemen surrounded him. Emma suddenly despaired of getting close enough to have a private word.

In fact, the thought of even attempting to speak to him while he was the center of attention suddenly seemed ridiculous.

With a wry smile on her lips to cover her unsettled emotions, she left her spot by the alcove and continued across the room.

She looked over at him standing in the midst of his friends as she moved toward a pair of open French doors that led to a lantern lit garden beyond. Her heart constricted as their eyes met and held, and even at this distance she felt the heat from his glittering black gaze.

It was too much. The music, noise, and people were all too much for her to take in while she felt so overwhelmed and unsure of herself.

With some difficulty, she pulled her gaze from his and

strode passed the other guests and stepped into the warm, soft air of the formal garden.

She took a deep breath and willed herself to calm down. But no matter how she tried, she could not shake the feeling that she was about to step off the edge of a cliff.

She continued to walk along the bricked path through the garden, aided by the half-full moon and the faerie lights scattered throughout the shrubbery, vaguely listening to the muffled noises of the party behind her.

"What?"

Emma froze upon hearing the surprised male voice. Glancing around in alarm, she determined the voice came from the other side of a bush to her left.

"I am quite serious, Tunbridge," she heard Penelope's shaky voice reply. "I do not wish you to give me any more jewels. It is insulting."

Penelope and Tunbridge! Emma put her hands to her fast-blushing cheeks, hardly able to think what to do, mortified that she had stumbled upon them this way.

"Insulting?" Tunbridge replied as Emma carefully and slowly began to turn around to go back up the pathway. "Explain to me how giving you jewelry could possibly be considered insulting." She heard the note of bewilderment in his deep voice.

"It is as if you are patting me on the head. You do not love me, and all these diamonds and emeralds are a poor way to make up for it."

In the ensuing silence, Emma held her breath as she tiptoed away, praying her friends would not decide to move and discover her. Stepping gingerly to avoid making any noise, she also prayed that Penelope was not about to get her heart utterly broken.

"My darling Penelope"—Tunbridge's tender, amused voice cut through the silence—"do you remember what you said to me on our wedding day when I tried to tell you of my regard for you?"

"Our wedding day? Ten years ago? I said lots of things,

but I do not recall anything specific," Penelope replied with a note of exasperation in her voice.

"Then I will refresh your recollection, my dearest goose. You looked me dead in the eye—and you were quite the loveliest thing I have ever beheld—and said, 'Just remember, Tunbridge, actions speak louder than words.'"

Emma was just far enough away to hear Penelope's soft reply. "Tunbridge, I do believe you are a bit of an idiot. Just because I said that does not mean that I never wanted to hear the words."

"I am not the idiot in this marriage, darling—you are the one who has been oblivious to how deeply I love you. And just to be clear, I shall give you jewelry anytime I please."

"Of course, my love" came Penelope's laughing, tremulous reply.

Hurrying up the pathway, Emma dashed a tear from her cheek and felt her heart soar for her friend's newfound happiness. She knew she was drawing near to the house, because she could hear the strains of a lilting waltz growing louder.

"Emmaline."

At the sound of her name spoken in that searingly familiar voice, Emma came to a stumbling stop and stared up at Jack in surprise.

The light flooding out from the open French doors behind him revealed stern, angled features.

"It is time that we talked, don't you agree?" he said.

Emma tried to swallow the lump in her throat so she could reply, but she was so overwhelmed that she failed.

It was strange, for she had wanted to speak to him so badly a short while ago, but now that he was standing before her, she could think of nothing to say.

She continued to gaze up at him and her heart ached with a tender joy as she marveled at the impressive man he had become. She had been unable to trust the boy he had been thirteen years ago. Could she trust the man who now stood before her?

She still hadn't regained the ability to speak, but Jack was not so afflicted.

"There is much I need to say to you, Emma."

"Yes?" she whispered, finding her voice at last.

"You were right to leave me that night, so long ago," he said without preamble. "It has taken me this long to realize what a callow youth I was then."

"No—" His words took her by surprise. This was not at all what she expected him to say.

"I was, Emma," he said, moving close enough for her to smell the faint smoky, woodsy scent that surrounded him. "And arrogant. I had no understanding of what I was asking of you when I wanted you to run away with me. Even worse, I was so arrogant that it never occurred to me that you would not wait for me after you did leave. I went back to Kingsmount and began to make other arrangements for our marriage. In truth, I wanted to punish you a little by making you wait," he said with a bitter, self-deprecating laugh before continuing. "I was so sure of our love, I thought you would wait forever, so it was a bitter blow when your uncle announced your betrothal to Charles Fallbrook."

"I am so sorry," she said, and her voice broke for a moment in remembered pain.

"Do not be," his arms slipped around her waist and he pulled her close. "I cannot regret the past anymore. We will never know how things could have been. I may have stayed a callow youth and you could have grown to hate me worse than you did when we met again."

Emma laughed a little at his dark humor. "I did not hate you, not really. I just never expected to feel what I did when we met again. It was as if you had the power to hurt me all over again, and I was frightened."

She felt the muscles in his arms flex, as she gazed up at him with her hands on his broad chest.

"Frightened? I would never have guessed it. I do not believe the girl I knew before would have kicked Monteford for his insult, dealt with his mistress with grace and good humor, nor ridden through the rain to warn me about his attempt to bribe my jockey. You have grown into the most amazing woman, Emmaline Wenlock Fallbrook."

She lowered her eyes from his. "I could not stand by and see you lose unfairly."

She realized her senses were being carried away by his nearness and the seductive emotion in his deep tone. She felt as if she was moving closer to the cliff's edge, and the tiny rational part of her mind asked again, *Can I trust him?*

She felt his warm breath on her temple as he continued. "I know that I spoke much too soon when I asked you to marry me at the Litchfield ball. I now understand because of the circumstance of your past that you are not ready to contemplate marriage—all I ask is that you not run away again."

Tears filled her eyes at the raw emotion in his voice. She suddenly knew with a clarity that seared her heart that instead of asking if she could trust him—she should be asking if she could she trust herself.

As the answer came, the last vestiges of regret and fear disappeared like vapor. The sweetness of this moment could not have been more perfect if it had happened when she was eighteen.

Finally, because of the love swelling in her heart, she felt completely, almost miraculously, free from the bleak pain of her past.

A tremulous smile came to her lips and she slipped her arms around his neck. "I'll never run away again."

An instant later, his lips were on hers in a half-fierce, half-tender kiss that took her breath away. She kissed him back with all the love and desire she had been keeping locked in her heart. The kiss deepened, and she pressed her body into his until her senses spun. His hands moved up and down her back and he said against her lips, "I love you, Emma."

Just as she was about to respond, the music whirling

around them stopped and the trilling notes of a fanfare
filled the moonlit air.

"Oh!" Emma said, her eyes wide with passion and surprised delight. "The duke must be ready to present the cup."
She did not want him to miss his moment of victory.

Jack smiled and kissed her again until the fanfare rose to
a resounding crescendo. Finally, he pulled back, took her
hand and raised it to his lips. "I suppose we had better go in
before they send a search party."

With a laugh Emma walked to the French doors with
him, her heart too full of joy for her to speak.

Just before they stepped back into the ballroom, Jack
stopped and turned to her, the desire in his eyes causing a
shiver to travel down her spine.

"I know this must seem sudden to you, my dearest Emmaline, but it is not to me. My soul has whispered your
name every night since I watched you walk away from me
on that dark road. As much as I told myself the opposite,
everything I have done since then—restoring Kingsmount,
my investments, my farms, building the racing stable—has
all been for you."

With heavy tears filling her eyes, Emma smiled up at
him. "I love you, Jack. I always have."

For a moment he stood very still, and then pulled her
back into his arms in a fierce embrace. "Marry me, Emma."

Burying her face in his neck, she said, "Yes."

Standing within the circle of his strong arms, she felt her
heart step off the cliff, and discovered it had wings.

SIGNET

REGENCY ROMANCE
from
Sharon Sobel

Lady Larkspur Declines
0-451-21459-5

Desperate to avoid an arranged—and
loveless—marriage, Lady Larkspur
fakes an illness only to fall
victim to her handsome doctor's
bedside manner.

Available wherever books are sold or at
penguin.com

Now available from
REGENCY ROMANCE

Marry in Haste and *Francesca's Rake*
by Lynn Kerstan
Together for the first time, two Regency classics star
heroines gambling on love, not knowing if they will
lose their hearts—or win true love.
0-451-21717-9

Miss Clarkson's Classmate
by Sharon Sobel
Emily Clarkson arrives at her new teaching position
expecting her employer to be a gentleman, and she's
shocked to find a brute. He's expecting a somber old
maid. And neither is expecting the passion that soon
overtakes them both.
0-451-21718-7

Available wherever books are sold or at penguin.com

Now available from
REGENCY ROMANCE

A Christmas Kiss and *Winter Wonderland*
by Elizabeth Mansfield
Two yuletide romances in one volume by "one of the best-loved authors of Regency romance" (*Romance Reader*).
0-451-21700-4

Regency Christmas Wishes
by Sandra Heath, Emma Jensen, Carla Kelly
Edith Layton, and Barbara Metzger
An anthology of Christmas novellas to warm your heart—from your favorite Regency authors.
0-451-21044-1

My Lady Gamester
by Cara King
A bankrupt lady with a thirst for risk sets her sights on a new mark—the Earl of Stoke. Now she has to take him for all he's worth—without losing her heart.

0-451-21719-5

Lord Grafton's Promise
by Jenna Mindel
A young widow and the man who suspects her of murder find their future holds more danger, surprise, and passion than either could have dreamed.
0-451-21702-0

Available wherever books are sold or at penguin.com

Now available from
REGENCY ROMANCE

Regency Christmas Courtship
by Barbara Metzger, Edith Layton,
Andrea Pickens, Nancy Butler, Gayle Buck
An anthology of all-new Christmas novellas to warm
your heart—from your favorite Regency authors.
0-451-21681-4

When Horses Fly
by Laurie Bishop
Cantankerous Lord Wintercroft has taken in Cora, a
poor relation and nurse, to live in his decrepit stone
castle and, eventually, to wed. But the nurse, herself, is
lovesick for Wintercroft's son, Alex.
0-451-21682-2

A Singular Lady
by Megan Frampton
Recently impoverished orphan Titania Stanhope must
marry money if she plans to survive. The Earl of
Oakley has money, but, in an attempt to keep gold-dig-
ging girls at bay, keeps it a secret. Then he meets
Titania, whose sharp wit and keen mind are rivaled
only by her lovely face.
0-451-21683-0

Available wherever books are sold or at
penguin.com